DEDICATION

For my older brother, Nate — because of the journey that you have embarked on, you have given me the courage to follow my path.

R. M. RADTKE

RM Radtke

Echoes of the Past

Westward Ho Series *(Book 1)*

Westward Ho Series, Book 1-Echoes of the Past © 2015 RM Radtke

Publisher: RM Radtke

Cover Design by: Jessica Richardson

Editing by: John Elek

ISBN-10: 978-1522906278
ISBN-13: 1522906274

CONTENTS

ECHOES OF THE PAST

ACKNOWLEDGMENTS

A special thank you to my husband Larry, for the constant encouragement you have given me. Also to my son, Frank, thank you for letting me use you as a sounding board. Your input, whether good or bad, used or not, was truly instrumental in getting my ideas and thoughts out of my head and properly placed onto the page.

I'd also like to thank Mindy. You have helped me in ways that I cannot begin to express. Our paths were meant to cross and I'm truly glad that they did.

CHAPTER 1

Taking a deep breath — her way of keeping the butterflies at bay — Kari opened the door and stepped inside.

It was her first day at her new job. She just accepted a position at Whispering Creek Senior Assisted-Living Home as an elder caregiver, and even though she was a little nervous, she was even more excited to get started. What she looked forward to most was, not only meeting all the residents residing there, she longed to hear their life stories.

Listening to older folks reminisce about their past had always been a treat for her, something she learned as a child. The seniors that she had cared for over the years had so many wonderful memories to share. Some, unfortunately, were not so pleasant, but every single one of them had one special memory that was the highlight of their life. Those were the stories that she desired and longed to hear.

Kari Davies, a single, middle-aged woman in her early forties, had devoted her life to helping the elderly. Working with senior citizens had become her daily life. Other than Alan, the only boyfriend that she had ever had, Kari made no room in her life to allow anyone in too close. She feared it would alter her path — a path that fate meant for her to follow.

An only child raised by her mother, in a single parent home, Kari never knew her father. He left before she was born. This did not stop her from having a happy and adventurous childhood. It wasn't until she became an adult herself, that she realize how much her mother must have struggled to make ends meet. The winter months were tough, but the summer months were what she really looked forward to — those were truly the best.

Summertime for Kari meant, staying with Aunt Gert up at her Lake House. She loved swimming in the river, which was no more that forty steps from the front porch, and reminiscing around the nightly bonfires.

The lake house was where she found real happiness. Spending every single day with just her mother and aunt, was absolutely the best time of her life. She loved listening to their stories, as they spruced up the house, both inside and out.

Over the years, Kari had come to realize it was because of these trips to the lake house, she was most comfortable being around people older than she, instead of those her own age. Her youthful years, sitting around all those bonfires, had groomed her for her destiny.

Once she heard the door close behind her, she headed straight towards the woman who was sitting behind the information desk.

"Good morning," she said to the heavyset woman. "My name is Kari Davies and..."

The woman, who had been shuffling papers around, obviously looking for something she had lost, abruptly stopped to see who had just interrupted her.

"Can I help you?" she asked, her tone sprinkled with a hint of annoyance.

"Yes, thank you, I am looking for a Mrs. Franks. Today is my first day working here and I need to report in." Kari said with a smile.

"First day, huh' she chuckled, 'boy oh boy, it's been a long time since it was my first day. Mmmm hmmm, ain't that right?"

"Excuse me?" Kari asked.

"Never you mind Miss Kari — you'll figure it out in time. Right now, you best hurry on down that hall — third door on the left is where you'll find her." She returned to shuffling her papers, then added,

"Mmmm Hmmm, I'm sure she is already waiting for you."

Smiling, Kari thanked the woman, and headed towards the hallway.

Lynnette Franks was sitting at her desk going over the morning schedule. Kari knocked on the open door to announce her presence as she stepped inside the room.

"You must be Kari," she said. "Come on in and have a seat. I'm Lynnette Franks, the Director of Whispering Creek."

Entering the office, Kari sat in one of the two chairs positioned in front of the Director's large mahogany desk.

"You look eager to get started," she said. "I like that. I think it will be a nice change of pace to have someone new around here. All of our employees have worked here a long time. So long, in fact, I think they just might transition themselves from workers to residents," she laughed.

Kari smiled, then offered, "It sounds to me like they must really enjoy their jobs. I mean, if nobody ever quits, that is."

"I'm not too sure about that — yet," Lynnette said, as she cocked an eyebrow at her. "I was just transferred here about nine months ago and I'm still learning their strengths and weaknesses. Well, enough about that; let's move on. I just have a couple of forms for you to fill out before I take you on the grand tour of the place and introduce you to everyone." Smiling, she gathered a small packet of papers and handed them to her.

Taking a few moments, Kari filled out the routine forms and handed them back. As she started to gather up her belongings, Lynnette picked up a black walkie-talkie and as she handed it to her, she said,

"This is for you. All personnel must carry one of these at all times while on the grounds. When you work with the elderly, anything can happen — at any time. This is so that you can radio for help or have Veeona call 911."

"Veeona? Who is that?"

"She is the lovely lady sitting at the front desk. I'm sure you spoke to her when you came in."

Nodding, Kari made a mental note of Veeona's name. Despite

the fact that she wasn't sure if Lynnette was speaking approvingly of Veeona or not, she found the woman to be quite charming — in her odd and quirky way.

"Alright Kari, everything seems to be in order here, are you ready for the tour?"

Rising from her chair, Kari replied, "Ready as the rain."

The tour took a little more than an hour. Lynnette had taken her around the grounds and introduced her to each of the residents. As they went along, she briefly explained which resident had special needs and how to handle them. Not every patient needed special attention, but there were a few.

As they arrived at room 237, and before Lynnette opened the door, she turned to Kari and said.

"This room belongs to Tess Parker. She is ninety-one years old and has lived here for well over fifty years now."

"Wow, I didn't think someone that young could move into an assisted living home, she had to be in her early forties when she moved in. Is she disabled?"

"No, not at all, she's just kind of...special. See, back in the '60's this place was kind of a halfway house, then in the late '80's, a group of investors purchased the property and converted into what is now. She's the only resident of the halfway house that never left."

"Why? What would make her want to stay?"

"I don't know, but what I do know is, she hasn't spoken to anyone in over twenty five years. She can still walk around on her own, she can feed herself, and she takes excellent care of her room. The only real problem we have with her is, she does not respond well to others. She wants to stay a recluse, but at Whispering Creek, we encourage everyone to interact with one another. So, with that being said, I am going to take you inside and introduce you to her. I want to warn you though, she may not respond well to you, but please don't be alarmed."

Kari noticed that as the director reached out for the door handle, her hand was trembling. Seeing how this woman was more nervous about the resident in room 237 than she was letting on, led Kari to take a second deep breath since arriving at her new job.

As the door opened, Lynnette chimed,

"Good morning Tess, how are we doing this morning?"

Using a light and cheery voice to announce her presence, she walked into the room with Kari right behind her.

"I brought someone in to meet you."

Upon entering the room, they found that Tess was sitting in a rocking chair near the only window. Glancing through the glass, Kari wanted to see what Tess was looking at and noticed that there wasn't much of a view at all. The only thing that she could see was just a few overgrown trees that lie just beyond a black decorative wrought iron fence, several yards away.

Tess never turned to look at the two women. Never letting on she even knew they were there. She just kept rocking in her chair, staring out the window. Lynnette kept her distance from the older woman and as she spoke, she kept her voice light and cheery.

"Tess, we have a new care assistant starting today. Her name is Kari Davies. I just wanted to bring her by to introduce her to you."

Shooting a look over to Kari, Lynnette mouthed the words, 'say hi'. Understanding and without hesitation, Kari took the lead.

"Hello Tess, my name is Kari. It's very nice to meet you," she paused, "I hope that we can become friends."

Still, there was no response. The elderly woman just continued to look out the window, rocking in her chair.

The director began checking over Tess's room and finding nothing out of place, motioned to Kari to head out the door. As they were leaving the room, she told Tess that someone would be back later to check in on her. Once the door closed behind them, Lynnette turned to Kari and said,

"Well, that went better than I expected."

"What did you expect?" Kari nervously asked.

"Well, Tess sometimes gets a little exasperated, and she likes throwing things. That is one reason why we make sure we serve all her meals on paper plates and she is only to use plastic utensils. Also, by no means is she ever to be given a knife — don't ever forget that Kari. The Kitchen is to have her meals cut into bite size pieces before they bring her food up, so there is no reason for her to need a knife — ever. And another thing, we do not permit her to have hot coffee or tea until she has finished her meal. You can serve it to her in either a paper or a foam cup only. Do you think you can remember all that?" she asked.

"Yes."

"I hope so Ms. Davies, I have seen the scars on the ones that don't."

CHAPTER 2

Lynnette Franks proceeded to take Kari around the grounds to meet the other employees, then presented her with a work schedule.

"Here is your badge; you will need to have this every day that you are here. If you lose it, there will be a hundred dollar fee for a replacement."

"A hundred dollars? Isn't that a bit steep?"

"Yes, it is, but it cuts down on the personnel from losing or forgetting them. It is crucial that you have it with you at all times. You will not be able to get from one wing to the other without it. Every entryway has a slide key lock on it and your badge is the key."

"Got it."

"Alright, let's get you settled in so you can start on your rounds, I'll show you where the locker room is so that you can change. Then I'll take you to over to meet Melva, she is our Assistant Head. You will report directly to her from now on."

"Assistant Head, Melva — got it."

Kari hoped that with all the mental notes she was making, none would slip her mind. She knew that with time, she would not have too much trouble remembering everyone's names; what worried her most was screwing up the residents that had the special needs.

Lynnette led Kari down the hall to the entrance of the locker room.

"Here is where you'll hang your coat, keep your purse, and change into your work attire. Make sure you lock your valuables in your locker and make doubly sure you don't lose your key to your lock. Go ahead and change your clothes, I'll wait here in the hall for you, and when you are done, we'll go find Melva."

Kari entered the locker room and proceeded to change her clothes. Locking her belongings in her locker and making sure to slip her key into her pant pocket, she left the locker room ready to begin her shift. Just as promised, Kari found Lynnette waiting for her in the hall.

"Are you ready to get started?"

"I'm ready as the rain Mrs. Franks."

"Please call me Lynn; we are not that formal around here. We like to make this place feel like home. After all, we are just one big happy family you know."

That made Kari smile — it had been a long time since she had been part of a family.

They rounded the corner and headed toward the assistant's main desk. Another grayed hair woman, with a stocky build was looking over some charts. As they approached, Lynn called out to her.

"Good morning Melva, how are you doing today? I brought you our newest addition."

Expecting to see Lynette wheeling in another senior resident, Melva was surprised to see that a rather attractive younger woman was accompanying her.

"You mean we actually have a new worker? Well, I'll be damned."

Smiling, Kari offered her a hello.

"Well, hello to you too honey. What is your name?"

"Kari. Kari Davies."

"Kari, that's such a lovely name."

"Thank you."

"So, have you ever worked in an assisted living home before?"

"Yes ma'am, I have."

As the two women began to exchange pleasantries and become acquainted with one another, the director turned to leave. As a departing note, she once again welcomed Kari to the team. She then instructed Melva to show her the ropes and to help her to get acquainted with their routine. Melva waved her off as she turned her full attention back to Kari — the newbie.

CHAPTER 3

Checking Kari out, from head to toe, Melva cocked an eyebrow and said,

"So now, you're my newbie huh?"

Stunned by the sudden change of this woman's tone of voice and her attitude, that had changed so dramatically as soon as Lynnette left the area, all Kari could do was just stare at her. Hoping that her jaw didn't physically drop open, Kari dug deep within herself to find and maintain her sense of professionalism. Deciding to keep her desire to dislike this woman in reserve, she wondered if she was strong enough to endure her torturous temperament.

"So, you've cared for the elderly before, huh?"

"Yes, I have." Kari responded as politely as she could muster. She focused on remaining professional, even though she was biting her tongue, hard enough to taste blood, to refrain from telling this woman a thing or two. By no means did she want her first day on the job to be her last.

"Good, cuz I ain't gonna hold your hand and babysit you. I am way too busy to worry about making sure you know your business."

"Well, all I need is a quick rundown of your procedures around here and a list of the residents that I will be tending to."

Kari too had changed her tone. As she spoke, she looked deep into the Assistant Head's eyes, hoping she was convincing enough in conveying that she wasn't intimidated, even though her insides were beginning to tremble — like the small tremors of a California earthquake. Then she added,

"Is that quick enough on the training?"

Cocking her eyebrow again, Melva said,

"Good enough for me."

With her eyebrow still cocked, a thin smile began to form across her lips as she continued,

"Come with me newbie, I'm going to give you a light load this week. You're only getting one resident to start with and that'll be Miss Parker."

"Miss Parker? Who is she again?" Kari asked.

"Room 237 — I'm gonna let you take care of her because she really doesn't need much help from anyone. Hell, she wouldn't tell you even if she did." Melva laughed.

"Oh, you mean Tess. Tess Parker, right?"

"Yep, the one and only," Melva replied, as she scooped up a file folder from the counter.

"Now here is her chart — read it over. Best if you can memorize it."

Walking down the hallway together towards room 237, Kari had a million questions she wanted to ask, but felt that it was best to hold off for a while. She didn't want to get Melva all riled up, especially on her first day.

As they arrived at room 237 and before the head assistant opened the door, Melva turned to Kari and said,

"Now, I'm sure that Lynnette gave you the rundown on Miss Parker. She is not to have any breakable cups or glass, and especially no knives. We only allow her to use; plastic forks, plastic spoons, paper plates, and plastic or paper cups. And, by no means is she to be given any hot beverages until after her meal has been eaten and cleared away. Got that?"

Kari nodded.

"I've been the only one for the last several years that has been able to take care of her and I want to see if she might take a liking to you. I need a replacement and I'm hoping that you will be it. I'm getting too old for this business and quite frankly, I'm getting rather tired of it as well."

Melva opened the door to Tess's room and stepped inside, with Kari right behind her.

"Tess — Miss Parker," she said as she sauntered into the room. "I've come to introduce you to your new aide."

Kari found that Tess was in the same spot that she was in earlier. She was still sitting in her rocker, rocking back and forth, looking out her window at the same nothingness of a view. Melva paid no attention to any of this as she walked right up and stood in front of Tess, trying to block her view of the outside but; Tess just continued rocking in her chair.

"Now don't give me that attitude, Miss Parker. You know the drill around here. Besides, I've been telling you for at least a year now that I've been want'n to retire, but I had to wait for a replacement. Well, now I got one, and I'm gonna use you to break her in."

Melva motioned for Kari to come over and stand next to her in order for Tess to see what she looked like. Even though she did not like Melva's tone of voice towards Tess, Kari did as she was instructed.

"Hi Tess — Miss Parker, we met about half an hour ago. I came in with Lynnette, remember?" There was no response.

Melva stepped away and began a brief routine inspection of Tess's room.

"I see that you dusted today Miss Parker. You did a mighty fine job too. I'll have Kari here come back with the vacuum; so these little dust bunnies can get picked up."

She looked over to Kari to make sure she got the hint and right on cue, Kari looked her in the eye and nodded.

"Lunch will be ready in about an hour Tess, but before it comes up, I think I'm going to let Kari take you out in the yard for some sunshine."

Tess didn't move a muscle. Like a zombie, she just continued to rock her chair, back and forth. Never letting on that she knew someone was even speaking to her.

"I know you probably don't want to go out there, but you know what I always say Tess, don't you? Sure, you do. I always say, too bad. Now you don't have to walk if you don't want to, that's fine. Kari can push the wheelchair and you will be back inside before you know it."

Rolling the wheelchair over to the rocker, Melva waited for Tess to get into it. The old woman didn't fight; she just took her time getting out of the rocker, and an even slower time getting into the wheelchair.

Not much of a fight today, Melva thought; *hope it stays that way.*

Handing control of the wheelchair over to Kari, Melva instructed her to take Tess out into the yard and push her around the path.

"By the time you get her back inside, her lunch should already be here on the table waiting for her."

Having a firm grip on the handles of the wheelchair, Kari started pushing Tess out of her room, down the hall and out to the yard, where the sun shone brightly on a beautiful spring morning.

CHAPTER 4

With the sun shining brightly and a warm, gentle breeze blowing, Kari slowly pushed Tess down the path. She had been trying to make small talk with the older woman, mainly because she felt awkward just pushing her around in utter silence. She knew Tess could hear, but what she really wanted to know was, why she hadn't spoken in over twenty five years.

"You know Tess, this is my first day on the job today, and so far, I think I'm going to like it here. The last place that I worked at, was nothing like this place at all," she said. "I used to work at a place called, Shepherd's Gate. I worked there for over ten years, but I really needed to get out of there. Why, you ask? Because, the staff was absolutely terrible! They were worse than terrible, maybe horribly horrific would be best to describe them. Those people didn't take care of the residents like they should have. Watching how they mistreated their charges, made me sick, and broke my heart. If it weren't for John and Lucy, I would have left there a long time ago. John King and Lucy Webber, they were my favorites. They were the residents that I took care of at Shepherd's Gate. Would you like to hear a little bit about them? They both told me remarkable stories about their lives, while we were together."

Of course, there was no response from Tess as Kari pushed her slowly around the path in the yard. Taking charge of the situation, she began to tell Tess a story.

"John was 94 years old, when I met him and a ward of the state. He was born just after World War I. He lost his father and his only uncle in that war. When he got older, he enlisted and fought in World War II. He received the Purple Heart and Silver Star medals during his tour and was given an honorable discharge for his services. I had seen a picture of him when he was a young man in the service and I'll tell you what Tess, if I had been born during that era and had known of him, I would have chased him down and made him marry me. Mmmm hmmm, he was a mighty fine looking hunk of a man."

Chuckling, she glanced down to see if she could get any response out of Tess. Unfortunately, Tess hadn't moved a muscle, she just sat there — enjoying her ride. Kari continued on,

"He told me how he had met his wife and how they had four children — three boys and one girl. The sad part about John's life was this; his wife, after thirty-four years of marriage, had gotten up one day and walked out on him. She told him that she was bored and wanted to have some resemblance of a life before she died. Not but two days later, as she was crossing the street, she was hit by a bus and killed instantly. Karma — swift justice, know what I mean?"

By now, Kari had made it to the backside of the path. She had been checking the layout of the land as she pushed Tess's chair around the yard, when she noticed the fence. She wondered why there was a fence wrapped around the entire perimeter of the property. She figured that in time, the answers to all of her questions about this place would be revealed. Trying not to get lost in her own thoughts, she continued her story about John.

"Poor John, his wife dies two days after leaving him and even though she had wanted a divorce, he made sure that she had a proper burial. He still loved her and it broke his heart when he heard about the way she died.

Did I tell you that he had four kids? Yeah, his only daughter — Colleen — I think that was her name, had turned eighteen earlier that year and had gotten married right after graduation. I guess that's what they did back in the day, people got married young.

Well, she got knocked up on her wedding night, poor thing.

Several months into their new marriage, her new husband, the wonderful drunken bastard that he was, waited until her belly started popping out — came home drunker than a skunk one night and accused her of cheating on him. He threw her around the house like a rag doll — from one end of the room to the other. Well, not only did the lousy bastard succeed in killing the baby, he ended up breaking Colleens neck in the process as well. Poor John lost his daughter and his grandchild and had another funeral to take care of.

That left John with his three sons — Robert, Steven, and John Jr. He referred to them as, Bobby, Moose, and Jr. Bobby was 23 years old, Moose 21 and Jr. was 19.

Three months after his daughter's funeral, the three boys had gone out to the local bar, on a Friday night. They were going to have a couple of beers and shoot some pool. At some point during the evening, Jr. had gotten into a fight with one of the local boys and Bobby and Moose had jumped in to help their little brother out. The fight got out of control, and a couple of pool sticks were broken and used as weapons — along with some broken beer bottles. During the ruckus, someone swung a broken, jagged edge beer bottle and stuck it into Jr's gut. Once his blood spilled all over the floor, the fighting was over. The police told John that, by the time the boys got him to the hospital, it was too late. He died before they could even get him into the operating room.

For the third time, in less than a year, John was planning another funeral. He told me that, if he had known that he would have had that many funerals in a single year, he would have bought stock in the dying business. I guess he meant funeral homes or cemeteries.

Anyway, now John had only two sons left, Bobby and Moose. The three of them were at the cemetery laying Jr. to rest, when John noticed that, only a few of the townsfolk showed up to pay their respects. He believed that they only came out because they were nosey and wanted to hear some gossip. He figured they wanted to hear about the bar fight and the gory details on how his poor son was killed. Sure, they felt bad for him, losing three family members so close to one another, but they were still nosey town folks with nothing better to do, than to nose around into other people's business. He claimed that he didn't *pay them no mind*, but to me, he said, '*Them's ignorant folks. They only feel better 'bout themselves when someone else is hurt'n.*'

It was at the end of his sons funeral that the pastor asked him if he could give him a ride home. John figured that since he hadn't been to church in a very long while, the pastor wanted to talk with him alone, probably to suggest grief counseling or encourage him to come back to the church and Sunday Worship. Poor John, he told me, that at the time, he was so numb from everything that had happened; he was just going through the motions of things and everything else was a blur. He said he barely remembered telling his two remaining son's, Bobby and Moose, to take the truck home and let them know that he'd be along shortly."

Kari had been almost back to the patio, but her story wasn't quite finished yet. She decided to slow her pace down in order to time the ending of her story with their arrival back to the door.

"His two boys got into the family truck and headed off for home. Five minutes later Pastor Tom and John got into the pastors station wagon and headed towards John's place as well. As the Pastor was talking with John, trying to make sense of the deep loss he must be going through, they found they were at a complete stop on the road, in a traffic jam. As they sat in the car trying to see what all the commotion was about, Sheriff Jones showed up and asked the pastor to step out. He got out of the car and the two spoke briefly, when John overheard the sheriff tell him that there was an accident up ahead and they may need his services. He watched the two men walk off, headed towards the accident.

Left in the car alone, he suddenly got a sick feeling in his gut and he could no longer control his emotions. The floodgates were about to be opened and there was no stopping his pent up sorrow from coming out. A single tear had managed to slip over the bottom of his eyelid, and slowly rolled down his cheek. When that single tear had reached the bottom of his jaw line and dropped onto his hand, there was absolutely no chance of him stopping the rest from falling. He first began to cry softly, covering his face with both hands and then, he did something that he had never done in his life — he began to sob uncontrollably.

He cried for his wife, his daughter, the grandchild that he never had the chance to meet and for Jr. Through his tears, he found that he began to pray, something he hadn't done in years. He wasn't even sure if he was doing it right, but he continued to pray like he had never prayed before. He begged God to not to make his gut feelings into a reality. He could not bear to lose another child.

As he continued crying and talking with God, the pastor came back to the car and he had the look of death all over him. John said that when the pastor got into the car, he just sat there, behind the wheel. He didn't move a muscle or said a single word — for at least five minutes. John desperately wanted to know what happened, but at the same time — he didn't. He decided that he would wait for the pastor to tell him, whenever he got around to it.

After several long and agonizing minutes, Pastor Tom finally turned towards John and said,

'It was Jerry Caldwell. He's not going to make it, he rolled his truck, and it wrapped around a tree.'

John hated to admit it, but he was thankful. Not happy that it was Jerry, but happy that it wasn't his boys. He then asked the pastor if he wanted him to drive home, *'You don't look so good Tom, maybe it's better if I drive. I'm pretty sure I can handle it.'*

John got behind the wheel of the car, turned it around, and took a different route home. When they arrived, relief washed over him when he saw his truck in the driveway. It was at that moment he realized how fearful he had been that something terrible might have happened to his last two sons.

After parking the car in his driveway, he asked the pastor to come in for some coffee, but the pastor declined, saying he had to get over to the hospital to be with the Caldwell family. But, before he left, he did tell John that he would like to take a rain check on the offer and that he would be back in a day or two.

Standing in the driveway, John waited until the pastors' car was out of view before he went into the house. Feeling broken up over the loss of his youngest son, he headed straight to the liquor cabinet, grabbed a bottle of whiskey, and poured himself a shot — a very large shot. He drank more than half of the bottle by the time he realized that his boys had come in and gone straight to bed.

That night, a horrible rainstorm came raging through — blinding lightning, deafening clashes of thunder and a hard wind that was blowing something fierce. John said that he had drunk so much that he had fallen asleep on the couch. At first, he thought that he was dreaming about a storm, but at some point, he woke up. His eyes opened just enough to see that the fierce winds had blown the front door wide open. He leapt off the couch and immediately, he felt the effects of the whiskey that he had consumed earlier. His head was pounding, throbbing as if an entire marching band were performing in there. He thought he was running to the door but, in actuality, his drunken stupor only allowed him to stagger. On very wobbly legs, he made his way to the door and attempted to close it. The wind was fierce and the gusts were so strong that it took enormous effort on his part to push the door against it and finally get it closed. It was then that he heard a loud crash and felt the house shake.

Fearing a tornado was coming, he headed straight to the boys' room. He needed to get them up and into the cellar. He tried to open the door, but it was jammed. He pushed with all his might, but it wouldn't budge. Fiercely he pounded on their door as he hollered out their names, but he got no response. Now he was absolutely out of his mind and in full panic mode. Completely frantic with fear, he ran outside into the pouring rain. The effects of the whiskey and his drunken demeanor had long since faded away, due to the adrenaline rush of fear that was now raging through his veins.

Heading to the side of the house, where the boys' room was located, with plans to break their window to get them out. He was hoping against all odds that he could wake them up in time. However, once he rounded the corner of the house, he stopped dead in his tracks after he had seen what happened. Everything that he had been hoping for, a mere moment earlier now seemed like a distant dream. His heart fell to the pit of his stomach and his once wobbly legs, bent at the knees as he fell to ground screaming. The noise of the storm could not drown out his pain; his ear-piercing shrieks could be heard at least two blocks away.

What John had seen when he rounded the corner of his house was, absolutely and completely incomprehensible. He found the tree that had once been a source of enjoyment for his kids when they were young, swinging from an old tire that he had tied to it years ago, had snapped in half and pierced the roof as if it were a spear. The weight of the trunk had collapsed a large section of the roof right in the center of their room. They never had a chance, it killed both boys instantly, while they slept. John had lost his entire family — all in one year.

Seeing the roof caved in and both his boy's bodies all mangled under the debris, made something snap inside. At that very moment, John quit the world.

He believed that by year's end, he too, would be dead. Not that he planned to do it himself — you know, like suicide. He figured that he would die, just as his family did — suddenly. He was waiting for death to come get him, just as it came for all of them. However, John didn't die, in fact, as I said earlier, he lived until he was 94. He told me he felt that life was like a prison sentence with no parole. Here his entire family didn't even have a chance to live and he, the one who wanted to die, had to live on, for what seemed like forever."

By now, Kari was nearing the patio door and as she looked down at her charge, noticed that Tess had not only been hearing her story, she was actually listening to it. This made her smile, because, she knew that a relationship was beginning between them. At that moment, she made up her mind as to what her new goal was, it was to try to get Tess to talk — sooner or later, she will talk.

"Wow Tess, we already finished with our walk, back at the building and I haven't even told you the story about Lucy yet. Well, I guess that'll have to wait for another time. There is a lot more to her story, it took her a long time tell me that one," she chuckled.

She noticed how Tess's shoulders had slumped down, ever so slightly, when she heard that story time was over. However, Tess didn't know that Kari wasn't finished with her story about John — yet.

"OK Tess, once we get you back into your room, I have to finish the story about John. It shouldn't take too long and by the time I finish, your lunch should be up. Does that sound good to you?"
Kari could tell by Tess's posture that that was a good deal.

Maneuvering the wheelchair through the doors and down the hallway, she managed to get Tess not only inside her room; she wheeled her right to the rocker. Kari asked if she needed any assistance getting up, but of course, there was no response. Tess merely got out of the wheelchair, of her own accord, and proceeded to sit down in her favorite chair — the rocker. Once she was situated, Kari pulled up a chair, set it next to her and went on to finish her story about John.

"Alright, where was I?" she asked. She noticed, but pretended not to see, that Tess was sneaking a peek at her once she began speaking.

"Oh yes, John ended up burying his two boys a few days after the big storm, but this time, the whole town had come out for the funerals. John was absolutely and completely numb, both inside and out. He wanted nothing to do with anything or anyone any longer, now he was just waiting for the grim reaper to show up and take him too. He somehow managed to make it through the day and began to believe that the reaper was coming for him during the night. After everyone left his home, late into the evening, he went off to bed expecting it to be his final time on earth. As morning broke and the sun rose that next day, John became angry. Every morning that he woke up and seen the light of the next day, he felt betrayed. He felt that God had forgotten about him — so, he decided to forget about Him. He walked away from his broken down house and left town — for good.

He lived on the streets for a while and eventually began selling newspapers from a corner stand and rented a room above a bar. Over time, he finally met another woman. Even though he loved her, he told me that he was never committed to her. He said that he was never going to allow his heart to be ripped out like that again — not by another human being.

Then one day, he had had a stroke and ultimately ended up at Shepherds Gate. From the first day he arrived, I was his only caregiver. For the first couple of months, he had to be fed, and let me tell you, he really hated that. I gave him some physical therapy, even though I wasn't allowed, and eventually he was able to feed himself. We used to talk for hours. In fact, I used to come in even on my days off, just to sit with him. He would tell me about the war and I would tell him about the current events. We used to talk about politics, religion and every now and again, he'd tell me about his family.

You know Tess, I knew he never got over losing his family, how could he? How in the hell could anyone get over something like that? All I knew was, I really liked John and I wasn't going to let anyone at Shepherds Gate abuse him — not on my watch. I hated working there, and as God as my witness Tess, I swore that I wasn't going to leave until the day he died — on his own that is. And that was when I met Lucy…"

The door opened and one of the kitchen staff came in with a meal tray. He quickly placed it on the small table just inside the door and then he was gone. Kari got up from her seat to get Tess's lunch set up for her and as she did, she said, "Your lunch is here Tess, I guess story time is over for today. Lucy will have to wait until tomorrow."

Tess got up from her rocker, moved to the small table, sat down and began to eat her meal. Kari wanted to sit with her, but she felt that she was being a bit too intrusive. As she headed for the door to leave the room, she noticed that Tess had turned to look at her. This gesture, not only surprised her, it solidified to Kari, that a real friendship was in the making. She carefully kept her excitement bottled up inside, but on the outside, Kari smiled. She then told her new friend that she would be back to pick up her tray and she would bring a cup of tea when she was finished eating. She promised her that she would stay for a little while and just sit with her until her shift ended for the day.

CHAPTER 5

The next morning, Kari arrived thirty minutes early for work. She was looking forward to the day's adventure, mainly because she loved taking care of the elderly. Seniors are rich with history and their stories of a time so long ago; seemed surreal. She had met and talked with so many senior citizens over the years and each one of them had the most interesting stories to tell. She marveled over the fact that, they had lived through the history that she had learned in her high school history class.

She could sit for hours listening to them, as they told story after story to her and never tire of it. Sometimes it was better, and juicier, than reading a book. Sometimes she would wonder, that when she got older herself and retired from this line of work, if she just might write a book about her own experiences. She had so many real life stories she could tell. Some were quite poignant and yet some were just off the charts thrilling and full of adventure. Pondering the idea for a few minutes, she smiled at the thought, then gathered her lunch bag as she opened the door and got out of the car.

Heading directly to the locker room to change into her work attire, she carefully hung her clothes in her locker and slammed the door shut. She put her lunch bag in the fridge, stopped in front of the mirror to check her appearance, then headed off to find Melva.

"Good morning Melva, how are you today?" Kari asked.

Looking up from her paperwork, Melva said,

"Good morning newbie, I see you survived Miss Parker yesterday."

"As a matter of fact I did, Melva. We had a nice long chat."
Melva's eyebrows went up in disbelief,

"Chat? Now you know that woman doesn't talk."

Feeling a bit deflated, Kari replied,

"I know. I did the chatting and she did the listening. But, I did get her to look at me when I left her room as she was eating lunch. That's something, right?"

"Well, since you seemed to hit it off so well with her, she will be your charge for today too."

"I'm only going to get one patient? Isn't there someone else that I can tend to as well?"

"Tess can be a handful at times and I don't want to rock the boat when it comes to her. If you had another charge to deal with and Tess needed more of your attention, then what would happen to the other charge?"

Melva had seen some of the light slip out of Kari's eyes and she felt bad about it.

"Kari, you'll get more charges in a few weeks, I just want you to concentrate on Tess for a while. Let her get to know you and you will become more familiar with her too. She's an old soul and she shouldn't be alone. I don't have the time anymore to tend to Tess's needs, especially since Lynnette took over."

Melva watched Kari's face to see if she understood what she meant and Kari didn't disappoint. Her facial expressions were as easy to read as a child's book.

"Alright Melva, I'll settle for just one charge. I can't believe that you want me to spend eight hours with her and do absolutely nothing else."

"I'll see what else I can find for you to do, how's that?"

A glimmer of light shot back into her eyes and she perked back up.

"That would be great. All right, I guess I'm off to 237."

Kari headed down the hallway towards Tess's room and as she walked, she thought that looking after only one person was actually a good idea. This way, she could devote all her time to Tess and maybe find out why she quit talking.

Arriving at room 237, Kari lightly knocked on the door, as she turned the handle and entered the room. Tess had already gotten up, made her bed and had dressed for the day. She was sitting in her rocker over by the window, just like the day before. However, she noticed that today, the wheelchair that was usually stored against the wall near the door, was placed at the rocker and ready for Tess to get into it. Kari smiled at how Tess was communicating with her. *Not bad for one day's work*, Kari thought.

"Good morning Tess. Did you sleep well last night?"

Kari walked on up to her charge and as she passed the small table, she noticed the food tray was empty.

"I see that you had your breakfast already. Would you like a cup of tea this morning?"

Nothing but silence came her way.

"I see you have your wheelchair here. How about we go outside and have tea on the patio. Then maybe we can take a stroll again around the grounds and I'll tell you a story about Lucy Webber."

Much to Kari's surprise, Tess stood right up from her rocker and sat in the wheelchair.

"Now *that* Miss Tess, tells me you are just itching to get outside," she chuckled.

CHAPTER 6

As Kari pushed Tess out onto the patio, she found that they were the first to be outside, alone to enjoy the morning together. The other residents were just getting up for the day, which meant that they still had to have their breakfast before they would start milling about outside.

Kari managed to get two cups of tea, in paper cups, out to the patio and the two sat in silence for a while just enjoying the sounds of the birds. The area was so peaceful and serene, Kari just didn't want to ruin it by talking.

Sitting in her wheelchair, Tess sipped on her tea as she gazed off into space. She didn't appear to be looking at anything in particular, just staring off to some distant place that she alone could see.

"Isn't it just beautiful here Tess? I could sit out here forever. It's so peaceful."

She waited to see if Tess would respond in some way, but she didn't. Tess just stared off into space and sipped her tea.

"I got an idea Tess, how about if we have lunch together — out here on the patio?"

That seemed to strike a nerve. Tess turned her gaze to Kari and for a brief moment, a very brief moment, a thin sliver of a smile crossed her lips. Kari knew that if she hadn't been looking at her when she spoke or if she had blinked at the wrong time, she surely would have missed it. Smiling back at her, she said,

"Alrighty then, lunch on the patio for the two of us it is."

Finishing her tea, Kari rose from her chair to throw her cup into the trash, noticing that Tess was not quite done. When she returned, she took the handles of the wheelchair and proceeded to push Tess down the walkway.

Kari made small talk for the entire first pass of the path. Talking about the trees, the squirrels and she asked tons of questions, which went unanswered. When they rounded the last corner, near the patio, Kari followed the path back down for a second trip.

"Would you like to hear about Lucy Webber Tess? She was another favorite person that I used to care for."

Tess sipped on her tea and then rested her elbow on the arm of the wheelchair, giving the impression she was comfortable and ready. As Kari pushed the wheelchair, she smiled knowing that Miss Parker was very interested in hearing a good story. She hoped that in time, Tess might feel compelled or inspired to tell her own story — one day.

CHAPTER 7

"Lucy Webber arrived at Shepherd's Gate three years before she died. She was eighty-seven years old when she passed, but in those three years that she lived there, she and I had become quite close. She told me all kinds of stories about her life and sometimes I wondered if she was pulling my leg with some of them.

Anyway, she was born in 1926, down in West Virginia. Her father had been a coal miner and she grew up in one of those coal-mining camps. She said that when she turned sixteen, she had to run away. Her daddy found her a husband and told her that she had to get married. She loved her daddy, he was a good husband to her momma and when he wasn't drinking, he was a good daddy too. She knew that he worked hard all day trying to provide for them, but she just wasn't ready to get married.

One day, while he was working in the mine, he told some guy on the pick line, that he could marry his little Lucy. It wasn't until after her daddy died that she found out that the guy was going to pay her pa a great deal of money for her. She told me that she didn't feel bad about her daddy not getting the money, but what surprised me was, she didn't hold a grudge against him for trying to sell her off in the first place. Could you imagine that?

The time that Lucy and I spent together was truly amazing. I spent most of it in complete silence, just listening to her tell the tale of her most treasured adventure and I must say Tess, it was truly a remarkable story.

It began in 1942 — just four months after WWII began. Things were hard to come by, especially for a young, uneducated girl, but she made do.

Her story began on a sad note. She told me that before she ran away, her mother had asked her one evening to go across the camp to get her father out of the Watering Hole — that would have been the closest thing to a bar, I guess. Anyway, she scurried on over to the Hole to get her daddy to come home. Upon entering the dingy, run down shack, filled with many of the mine workers, she spotted her father right away. He was drunker than a skunk and full of piss and vinegar. She had walked up to him and put her hand on his arm to tell him that momma sent her to get him but, he shook her hand off his arm and then whacked her across her face.

"Get out of here you li'l whore," he yelled at her.

She went flying backwards and ended up on some old guys lap. He didn't waste any time slipping his hand up her dress and putting his dirty fingers on her privates. She screamed and tried to get away, but the old guy just held her firm until his fingers found what he was looking for. All the while that his fingers were busy, he was rubbing her bottom over his groin, hoping to get a quick hard-on.

Screaming and crying, she managed to wiggle her way off the creepy, dirty old man's lap and went running from the Hole. As she ran out the door, all she heard was an eruption of laughter coming from inside the place. The laughter echoed in her ears, making her sick to her stomach, as she ran towards home.

Four days earlier, she had turned sixteen and she hadn't even had a boyfriend yet. So having that dirty old man touch her in such a way — absolutely revolted her. As she crossed the camp sobbing, she had made up her mind that she was never going to marry a man that worked in the coal mines. To her, those men were nothing but dirty, filthy old men that were drunk most of the time and they didn't make a whole lot of money either. Deciding in a blink of an eye that she was going to run away, she wiped the tears from her face and headed for home.

It didn't take her long to plan her escape. All she had to do was wait until the following week when her daddy would, once again, go off to the Water Hole and spend most of his paycheck at the bar. She had already packed some clothes in a haversack and hid it out back. When darkness fell, she slipped out of the house, grabbed her hidden bag and off into the night she went.

Having no real destination in mind, except for heading west, her first night out on the road she just spent walking. She wanted — no, she needed, to get as far away from the coal mine as she could. She walked along the road and when she would either see the headlights of a truck or hear tires crunching on the gravel road, she would jump into the bushes on the side of the road and hide until they passed.

As soon as dawn broke, she found that she was near an apple orchard. She could smell the sweet scent of the apples on the trees. Slipping over the fence, she gathered up some of the apples on the ground and put them in her sack. She figured that she could eat them as she walked to where ever it is she was going. By now she had been walking for hours and had gotten very tired. She looked around for somewhere to rest, when she found a clearing in the brush. The clearing was still near the road, but she knew that if she were lying down — nobody would be able to see her. She figured that by traveling at night, she would have a better chance at getting away. So, she slept as best as she could, until dusk.

When her second night's journey resumed, she claimed to have walked at least fifty miles. Now I don't know much about West Virginia or what times were like back in the forties, but I would think that a young girl all alone at night would have been really scared to be out there — especially alone."

Kari notice that Tess was very relaxed and enjoying not only the fresh air, she was very much into the story about Lucy. As they reached the back side of the path, there was a bench that overlooked what used to be a flower garden. With all the cutbacks that the company was going through, there just wasn't enough funds to invest in plants or flowers for the garden. The grounds keeper had let the garden go wild and was probably going to fill it with grass seed in the fall.

31

She positioned the wheelchair at the end of the bench and angled it so that they would be sitting next to each other. Tess had too been looking at what remained of the flower garden and to Kari, the sadness that she saw in Tess's eyes, spoke volumes.

"I bet that was a beautiful flower garden back in the day, right Tess? I wish there was something we could do to spruce it back up."

Noticing how Tess perked up just a tad had made her wonder if she could get her to interact, if they attempted to clean up the flowerbed.

As Kari was lost in her own thoughts, Tess had turned her attention away from the flower bed and focused it on her. Seeing her, as if for the first time and taking in all of her features. Tess wanted to remember this young woman's face.

Having the sense of being watched, Kari turned to face Tess. Looking into each other's eyes, Kari savored the moment and chose not to say a word. They just looked at each other and then something remarkable happened. The corner of Tess's lips started to lift and soon it became apparent that she was smiling at her. This was not just any old smile, or in Tess's case, a sliver across her lips. It was a full fledge smile that brightened up her face, one that removed at least ten years from her. Kari was so excited that she couldn't help but say so.

"Oh Tess, you have such a beautiful smile. You should do that more often sweetie, it makes you look younger too. Uh, not that you look old, oh man, I think I should just shut up."

Laughing inside, Tess let her smile get even bigger. If Kari were a betting girl, she would have bet that this moment might have made some headway in breaking down Tess's tough exterior. And now, more than ever, she wanted to get the real story of Tess out of her.

"OK, where was I?" Kari continued, "Oh yeah, Lucy had walked fifty miles when finally, she came into a small town.

Across a field, she had seen a barn and thought that maybe she could sneak inside of it. She knew that there would be hay inside and the thought of lying on something softer than the ground appealed to her besides, being inside a building she could at least try to get some much needed rest. She surveyed the area and concluded that there was no one around. As she quietly snuck onto the property, she noticed that the farmer was out in the field running his tractor. She managed to get into the barn unnoticed and after climbing up into the hayloft; she took one of her apples from her bag and began eating it. She fluffed some hay into a pile and fashioned a makeshift bed. Positioning the pile near a small opening in the wall where the boards didn't quite meet, she felt a little more at ease about being in the loft. She liked the fact that the light was shining through and she hoped to use it to her advantage. With her being able to peek through the hole, she would be able to judge when the day would turn to night. As she rested in the hay enjoying her apple, it didn't take long for exhaustion set in and soon she had fallen fast asleep, her apple left unfinished.

A noise from down below woke her from her sleep. It must have been getting late because she could see the farmer putting his tractor away for the night. Hidden by a couple bales of hay, she sat as quiet as a church mouse — not moving a muscle. The farmer, moving about with his business, never knew he had a stowaway hiding out in his barn.

Waiting until the stars were shining brightly up in the dark evening sky and as soon as the lights turned out in the farmer's house, Lucy bravely climbed out of the loft and snuck off the farm. Refreshed from her long nap, she was grateful that she had a warm, safe place to stay. She really needed the rest after walking so much the night before.

A few days had passed when, one evening, she happened to come upon a pond. Looking around to make sure that she was alone, she decided that it was time to take a bath and change her clothes.

As she had stripped down, she folded each piece of her clothing and carefully placed them in a neat pile near the edge of the pond. Standing there, naked in the moonlight, she slowly entered the water. As she swam around and enjoyed herself, skinny-dipping under a full moon, she heard some rustling in the bushes. Looking around but seeing nothing, she became afraid that it was a wild animal. She searched the shore for a large stick or branch or something, anything that she could use as a weapon to try to protect herself, but the shore was void of any such things. Slowly she emerged from the pond, but now, she felt more exposed than just being wet and naked. As she made her way to where she left her pile of clothes, two young men came out of the brush. One guy was tall and thin and the other, round and chunky.

"Well, well, well. What do we have here?" one of them said.

Lucy tried to grab some of her clothing so she could cover up, but the second guy had beat her to it. All she could do was wrap her arms around herself and try to cover up what she could.

"What's your name little lady?"

Not knowing them, nor trusting them, she decided to lie.

"Carol" she told him.

"Well, Carol — what are you doing down here in the pond — alone — and naked?"

"I was just relaxing in the water — needed to wash the dust from my feet."

"Your feet? Then tell me why the rest of you is buck naked?"

"Never you mind that mister; it's not your concern. Would you mind telling your friend over there to give me back my clothes? It's getting kind of chilly standing here."

Standing there smiling, the stranger just stared at her as she dripped water puddles at her feet and shivered in the night's cool breeze. Shooting a look over to his friend, he ordered him to throw her something small, so she can at least dry off. The one holding her clothing, decided to throw her a handkerchief, the one that she uses to tie on her head.

Turning her back to them, Lucy took the kerchief and began to dry herself off as best as she could. Still wet and cold, she opened the handkerchief and used it to cover her small breasts, as she turned back towards the two young men.

"Now can I have the rest of my clothing?" she asked them.

"Not so fast, Missy. I think that me and Buster here, might have something better in mind. I think it just might warm you up in the process too."

Even though Lucy never had sex before, she knew that these two had something awful in mind. She figured he meant they were planning to rape her, but she wasn't going to make it easy for them either.

"Well, all I have to ask you is this — have you ever fucked a girl before?"

A shocked expression came across the thin one's face and his sidekick Buster was no better.

"Listen to that dirty mouth you have. Hey Buster, have you ever heard the mouth of a sailor on such a divine creature before?"

"Can't say fer sure Jack, but she sure does have a way with words, don't she?"

"Mmmm hmmm, I've been surprised twice this evening. First by a beautiful naked lady, just asking for a deflowering and now by a dirty mouth that needs some cleaning."

He looked over at Buster and they both started laughing.

Buster held back and let his friend head on down to the shoreline. By the time he was half way there, Jack already had his shirt off and his pants unbuckled. Lucy had been desperately looking around for something to use as a weapon but, even though the moon shone brightly in the night's dark sky, she couldn't find a thing. Grabbing her roughly, Jack whispered in her ear,

"I'm going to show you something you ain't ever going to forget sugar."

"You ain't man enough to show me noth'n," she shot back.

"Get over here you little whore."

Having a firm grip on her arms, he spun her around and dropped her down, face first onto the sandy shore and within seconds, he began to rape her from behind. It hurt like hell as he penetrated her, but she wasn't going to give him the satisfaction of knowing it. She laid there cringing, trying like the devil to make sure that she didn't let her tears flow. The agonizing pain that she felt all the while he rocked back and forth, trying to get his jizum out, was excruciating.

She opened her eyes for a brief moment and that was when her sight rested upon a nearby rock. She stretched out her arm as far as she could, but the rock was just out of range. With every thrust that her rapist made, she gently pushed herself forward along the soft surface of the sand and soon it was within reach. Stretching out her hand once more, her fingertips finally felt the roughness of the rock. Grasping it, she drew it into the palm of her hand and slowly she pulled it in close to her body, waiting for the right moment to strike. Then she heard him call out to his friend,

"Buster, get your pants down and get ready. Soon as I pull out, you get in."

Buster came running down to the shore, dropping all her clothes right next to her head. He was so nervous and clumsy that, he couldn't get his pants undone. He was still fumbling with this belt buckle just as Jack reached his climax.

Waiting for the right moment, Lucy felt Jack pull his dripping limp penis from her and with moves like a ninja; she bolted upright and pounded both boys in the head with the rock. She had hit them so hard that not only did she knock them out; she split both their heads open at the temple with a single blow.

She wasn't sure if she killed them, and she really didn't care either. Terrified they may get back up and beat her to death, she grabbed all her belongings and ran silently into the night — naked."

CHAPTER 8

Kari sat quietly for a moment, giving Tess a moment to let Lucy's story sink in. Even as she repeated the story that Lucy had told her several years ago, Lucy's rape troubled her deeply. It just didn't seem right to continue on with her story after talking about something so brutal, even if it happened many years ago.

Kari looked over towards Tess and noticed that she once again was staring off towards the dilapidated flowerbed, but this time she had an irritated look on her face. Did the rape of Lucy trigger something within her? Was the visualization of what Lucy went through too much for her? Kari wasn't sure, but she figured that if she continued on with the story, Tess would signal her in some way to let her know she had had enough. After a few moments of silence, Kari resumed telling Lucy's story.

"With all her belongings clutched in her arms, Lucy ran and ran, long into the night. It was only when she felt a pain in her side did she feel that she had run far enough away from the two rapists. Feeling somewhat safe, she allowed herself a few minutes to jump into the brush on the side of the road so she could quickly slip on some clothing. She was able to get the rest of her belongings crammed into her haversack and soon she was on her journey once more.

Not knowing where she was going, Lucy soon started feeling depressed. It wasn't long before her depression turned into feelings of being homesick. Oh, how she longed for her mother, wishing that she were with her as she walked along on that long, dark, gravel road. As she walked through the night, quietly she began to cry and with tears streaming down her cheeks, her thoughts kept going back to those two guys that raped her. She desperately tried to remember the name of her rapist. She knew the other one's name was Buster, but for some reason she just couldn't remember the dirty bastard's name that had raped her. Writing it off to shock, she knew one thing for sure, she would always remember what he looked like. She made a mental note of the town and the name of the road, because she secretly wanted to come back and take care of those boys — no matter how long it took.

After some time, she made it to Ohio and it was there that she managed to get a job in some coffee shop, waiting on tables and washing dishes. I'm not sure how she ended up in Ohio — Lucy was a little fuzzy on some parts of her story, but working in that diner was how she managed to eat most days. She worked there for about a year when they hired a new girl. She was tall, slender, and very beautiful. I think her name was Lee or something like that. Lucy and the new girl had become close friends, mainly because they were both runaways. Lucy, by then, was seventeen and Lee, was either eighteen or nineteen.

As the two spent time getting to know each other better, Lucy found out that Lee had a plan. A plan to move on to Hollywood and become a movie star, but Lucy had no plan. The two had spent every day together, working in the coffee shop, talking about what they were going to do in life and eventually they moved in together to save more of their money. It didn't take long for Lee's plan to become Lucy's plan too. The pair was now — Hollywood bound.

Traveling together was a little bit safer too, one could always keep watch while the other slept and with Lee's ravishing good looks, getting a ride was easy as well. They hitched a ride with a trucker, headed for Chicago. They stayed there for two days and something bad happened to Lee. Lucy wouldn't tell me what happened, she would just start crying and then we would have to talk about something else for the rest of the day. What I do know is this — she really loved that Lee. She would have done anything for her, all Lee needed to do, was ask.

Their journey was a long one. I think it took them better than six months of traveling. Oh, I'm getting ahead of myself. I don't want to ruin the story for you. All right, I'll start with the part where Lee got hurt and Lucy was tending to her wounds. That evening, when darkness came, the two slipped out of town as quietly as they came into it. Lucy led them through the town and down towards the train station.

"Lucy, we don't have enough money for two tickets."

"Who said we need tickets?"

"What? Then what are we doing at the train station?"

Lucy had looked her straight in the eye and asked,

"All I want to know Lee is, can you run?"

Looking back at her friend, Lee nodded yes.

"Good. We are going to hide in the bushes down the tracks and when the train starts to leave, we are going to jump into one of the open cars. Now, what I want you to do is this, you start going down the track, but make sure you stay in the shadows. I don't want anyone to see you."

"What are you going to do?"

"I'm going to walk along the train and find an empty car and mark it with this piece of chalk that I stole a long time ago. Then I'm going to count how many cars it is from the engine, so we won't miss it as it is passing us in the dark."

Lee slipped into the darkness and headed out into the field, while Lucy headed towards the train. Lucy had been nearly caught a couple of times by the railroad men that were checking the train for freeloaders. She opened one railcar door and found a wino sleeping inside. Eventually, she found a car that the two could jump into, when the time came, but first she had to find out where the train's destination was. After she counted the cars from the engine to the one that she marked with chalk, Lucy headed towards the rail station. Before entering, she swatted her clothes down, trying to get the road dust off them. Using her hanky, she wiped as much of the dust off her shoes as she could. Hoping that she looked presentable enough to pass as a purchasing passenger, she entered the depot building. Without any hesitation, she walked right up the man sitting in the ticket booth. As politely as she could muster, she asked how much a ticket would cost for the train that was sitting out front on the tracks.

"Depends, where it is you are going little lady?"

"Well, where is that train headed for and when does it leave?" she asked.

"That one is going as far as New Mexico and it will pull out in about fifteen minutes."

Not sure where New Mexico was, she opted for a state that she knew about.

"Hmm, is it going through Oklahoma City?"

"Sure honey, it will be making a stop in Oklahoma. Is that where you're headed?"

"Depends on how much that ticket is, I reckon."

"It will cost you twenty five dollars. Do you want one?"

Knowing that she didn't have that much money, she pretended that she was thinking about it. She opened her bag and started rummaging through it, hoping that her acting was convincing enough. She then glanced up at the ticket man, told him that she had better wait a few more weeks, and save some more cash. Nodding his head, he wasted no time in turning his attention back to the newspaper he had been reading before she stepped up to his window.

Lucy walked out of the station and headed towards the main road. Once she was out of view of the depot, she made her way into the darkness and then slipped into the field, then backtracked towards the train tracks. Eventually, she found Lee sitting in the weeds where the two waited for the train to roll by.

"How long do we have to wait Lucy?"

"It should be starting up in a few minutes. The car we want is

thirty-four cars behind the engine. We'll have plenty of time to get on it."

"Oh good. So tell me, what happened in there?"

"Nothing, but if we had fifty dollars we could have ridden on the train the right way."

"Fifty-dollars, really?"

"Yep, twenty-five dollars apiece, but that would only get us as far as Oklahoma. This way, we can go all the way to New Mexico. Have you ever heard of New Mexico, or better yet, do you know where it is?"

Being that Lee had more schooling than Lucy did, she knew a little bit more about some things than her. Besides, Lee also knew how to read a map and Lucy managed to get her hands on one back at the train depot.

CHAPTER 9

As the train started rolling down the track, the two girls ran through the weeds, down the hill and towards the train.

"Now remember,' she hollered over her shoulder, 'if you jump on first, grab hold of the side rail next to the door, hold your hand out so that you can pull me in and I'll do the same."

"OK Lu — Just don't leave me behind — please."

"I will never leave you Lee, if you don't make it on the train, I'll jump off. OK?"

Lucy began counting the cars and when she got to twenty-nine, she grabbed Lee's hand and they began running in the same direction as the train. Looking over her shoulder, Lucy searched for the identifying chalk mark she made. As it came into view, she sprung like a cat and jumped into the empty rail car. Grabbing hold of the side rail, she leaned out as far as she could and yelled to her friend to run.

"Hurry up Lee, get the lead out of your ass!" she hollered.

Lee had been running as fast as she could and was almost out of breath but, low and behold, she kicked it up a notch and as if the devil was burning a hole in her panties, she flew like lightning. Their hands met in the darkness and as soon as Lucy felt her grip, she pulled with all her might and Lee plopped into the moving rail car.

Both girls were out of breath, lying on the floor and gasping for air. They looked at each other and an out of breath Lee said,

"Get the lead out of my ass? Is that what you said to me?"

"You were losing ground fast and I needed something that would make you speed up. It worked, didn't it. You're here on the train ain't ya?"

Too winded to respond, Lee just looked at her friend and within moments, both girls started laughing uncontrollably.

Lucy was the first to get up and check out the inside of the rail car. There was nothing much to find because, there wasn't anything inside but some loose hay scattered on the floor. She began to gather it into a pile, and then shoved it all into one corner. Cold and tired, the girls huddled together, sitting on the pile of hay and soon they both fell asleep, listening to the rhythm of wheels riding along the tracks.

As daylight came upon them, Lucy pulled out the map, opened it up and began to look it over. After several minutes of staring at the lines on the page, she ended up handing it over to Lee.

"Can you make out where we are with this?"

"I can sure try. Where'd you get it?"

"I picked it up back at the train station. The ticket guy was reading his paper, he seemed rather engrossed in what he was doing and I'm pretty sure he never even knew I was in there until I stepped up to his window." She laughed.

"That was kind of dangerous Lu, what if you got caught?"

"Well, I didn't," she snorted, *"And we needed the stupid map right?"*

Lee wasn't going to start arguing with her, because she knew that when Lucy makes her mind up to do something, Lucy just does it.

"Alright, don't get your panties all in a bunch," Lee shot back.

Lee then, quickly turned her full attention to the map. Looking it over carefully, Lee hoped she could make heads or tails out of it, when she asked,

"You did say that this train is going to stop at Louisville right?"

"Yeah, so?"

"All right, I'll start with Oklahoma and work backwards to find where we are right now. Can you look out the door and see if you can find any signs?"

"Uh no, not really. I don't want to get caught now. The engineer has mirrors on his car so he can see people like us, sticking our heads out just to read a sign. You know that if he sees us, he will stop this train right here and now don't you?"

"No, I didn't know that. So how are we going to see where we've been then?"

"I suppose we will have to wait until we stop. You do know that we have to get off this train when it stops, right?"

"No. Why do we have to that?"

Lucy rolled her eyes and explained to Lee that the conductor checks every car, every time that the train stops.

"They make sure that there aren't people like us, stealing a ride."

"That means that we have to jump back on again?"

"Yep, the problem is, if this train stops someplace during the daytime, we're going to have to wait until dark to get back on one."

That was exactly what Lee didn't want to hear. She barely made it on this time, what will happen the next time, she thought.

Looking at her watch, Kari realized that it was almost past lunchtime.

"Oh for heaven's sake Tess, I've talked so much that we almost missed lunch."

She told Tess to hang on because she had to hurry to get her back inside, so she could eat.

"If you don't mind Tess, I'm going to bring you back to your room and get you situated first, and then I will grab my lunch and come eat it in there with you. I know that I said we would eat outside, but the sun is getting too hot."

Looking for some sign of approval on Tess's face, Kari was a little disappointed that there wasn't any. Tess was as silent as a stone wall. Kari continued as if there was no problem, hoping that she didn't upset her charge Tess. As she wheeled her back towards her room, she watched Tess's body language, looking for signs of anger or anything she should worry about. Fortunately, there were none, or at least she didn't detect any.

As they entered the room, they had seen that Tess's lunch had been delivered and was placed on the table, waiting for her. Wheeling her in, Kari said,

"Wow, looks like we made it back just in time huh? I hope you're hungry."

She locked the brakes on the wheelchair and waited to see if Tess needed help getting out of the chair. Tess did not. She managed to rise from the wheelchair without assistance then went into the bathroom, to wash up for lunch. By the time that Kari folded the wheelchair and set it out of the way, Tess was out of the bathroom and headed for the table. Once Tess was seated at the table and before she left the room, Kari helped Tess get her plates situated so she could eat with ease.

"Alrighty then, looks like you got everything. Go ahead and start eating, I'll be right back."

Kari stepped towards the door and slipped out of the room.

CHAPTER 10

After retrieving her lunch from the employee refrigerator, Kari started heading back to room 237. Melva just happened to swing around the corner, spotted her in the hallway and asked how things were going.

"Things are going fine. Tess and I are hitting it off really well."

"That's good to hear, so where are you headed right now?"

"I was going back to have lunch with her. I told her that I thought we should have lunch together."

Melva was surprised by the newbie's news then asked her,

"You don't have anything sharp in that lunch bag of yours, do you?"

"No, the only lethal thing I have in here is a tuna fish sandwich."

Chuckling, Melva shook her head as she stepped away to finish her rounds.

"Enjoy your lunch."

"Thank you, I will."

Kari tapped on the door to room 237 before she walked in. She found Tess sitting at the small table with all of her food still in front of her. It was obvious that she had been waiting for Kari to arrive, so they could eat together.

"I'm sorry it took so long to get back here Tess and I'm sorry we didn't stay out by the patio either. I just figured that with the sun beating down so hard on you, it would be better to get you into some shade. Then I ran into Melva in the hallway. She wanted to know how things were going between you and me. Whew wee, that Melva sure can be long winded. Mmmm hmmm, I kid you not, that woman sure asks a lot of questions you know."

Kari began chuckling to herself and then said,

"I know what you're thinking, *look who's calling the kettle black* — the queen of questions. Well ha ha."

Tess didn't laugh.

As she pulled her sandwich out of her bag, Tess picked up her plastic fork and they both had a nice quiet lunch — together.

CHAPTER 11

"Are you ready for another cup of tea?"

Kari asked as she watched carefully for a sign from her charge, to see if she wanted a cup. Tess did not hesitate in giving her one either. She gently slid her tray to the center of the table to signal that she had finished eating and that was all Kari needed to know.

Removing her food tray, Kari stepped out of the room to retrieve two cups of tea. Upon her return, she found that Tess had gotten back into her wheelchair and was waiting for Kari to take her back outside.

"Well, look at you," Kari said approvingly.

"I guess you want to go for another walk huh? Well, I'm not sure how to get you, this wheelchair and these two cups of tea outside all at the same time."

That was when a remarkable thing happened. Tess raised both her hands, motioning to Kari to hand her the two cups of tea. Shocked and surprised, Kari asked,

"Are you sure you can hold both of these?"

Tess's hands remained in the air waiting for Kari to place the cups into them.

Once they were back outside, Kari decided to push her down the path so they could sit on the furthest bench at the end of the yard. They sat for a while just enjoying the breeze and sipping on their tea when, Tess turned to Kari and just stared at her. Kari looked into her eyes and that was when she first noticed how blue they were. Her charge may be ninety-one years old, but her eyes looked as young as someone in their twenties. They were bright, full of life, and as blue as the ocean. She wondered what Tess had looked like back in her youth. She really was itching to get her life story out of her, but she remembered that not everyone wants to share their story — especially to a perfect stranger. *Baby steps*, she thought to herself, *baby steps*.

"Are you ready to hear more about Lucy?"

That was when the corner of Tess's mouth turned upward, forming into something close to a smile, and that was the only sign that Kari needed for confirmation to continue.

"OK, let's see, I think I left off with the girls on the train. They were trying to read the map and see if they were heading in the right direction. They had a long way to travel and they both prayed that when the train had to stop, that it would be nighttime.

At some point, they made it past Iowa. They rode that train for a long time. They weren't sure if the engineer knew they were stowing away on his train or if the guy was just stupid, but whatever the reason was, they didn't care.

Eventually, the train stopped in some dirty little town in Nebraska and they had to get off the train. Dusk was upon them, but they managed to sneak behind the train depot and emerge on the other side without detection.

As they walked through the town, there was a scent of food cooking in the air. With their stomachs empty and rumbling, they walked further up the road to find that a corner diner was advertising hamburgers and coney dogs for five cents.

"Lucy, do you think we have enough to get a hamburger? We could probably share one."

"Let's stop over here so I can count our money and then we'll see about eating."

"I'm starved and I know you have to be too. We haven't eaten for two days. Maybe we can stop in and see if we can work off our meals. You know, like wash the dishes or clean the kitchen or something."

Lee looked hopeful, but Lucy wasn't too sure that the plan would work. Just because their old boss, back in Ohio, used to do that for some people, didn't mean that anyone else would.

"Let's just see Lu please? Besides, my feet hurt and I need to sit down."

"Oh alright, let's go in, I think we can spare five cents for one hamburger. Maybe it will come with French-fries too."

As they walked down a near deserted street, they headed for the corner diner. They passed the local bus stop and that was when they notice a man waiting for the bus. His clothes were filthy and it looked like he hadn't bathed in months. As soon as he had seen the two girls, he perked right up.

"Where you gal's headed?" he asked.

Lucy whispered to Lee to ignore him and just keep walking. The girls crossed the street to avoid the bus stop all together, when they heard,

"Hey, what are you two deaf or sum thin?" He spoke with a lisp due to his front teeth had rotted right out of his mouth.

The girls didn't want to break into a run to let him know that they were scared, but they did quicken their pace a bit. Finally, they reached the diner just to find that the doors were locked and the place was closed for the night.

"Oh Lucy, they're closing and I'm so hungry. What are we going to do now?"

Lee, the emotional one, began to cry. Seeing the tears run down her friend's face, Lucy didn't hesitate to react. She started pounding on the locked door of the diner.

The owner, a large, round, white haired older man came to the door and opened it.

"I'm'a sorry ladies, we are closed for da evening. You com'a back tomorrow – OK?"

He smiled at them and began to close the door on them. Lucy slipped her foot in the door and quickly said,

"No, it is not OK," she insisted. She changed her tone from irritation to pleading, then said, *"Please, there is a strange man at the bus stop and we are afraid. Please can we come in until he is gone?"*

The elderly man opened the door and stepped out onto the sidewalk so he could get a better look at the bus stop. Sure enough, he saw the drifter looking at the two girls.

"OK, you com'a inside."

He let the girls enter and locked the door behind them.

"Com'on, you two, tak'a seat. You want some water?"

Lucy looked at Lee and they both eagerly said yes. In the kitchen was the wife of the owner. They could hear her banging the pots against the sink as she was washing them out. This gave Lucy an idea.

"Sir, thank you so much for letting me and my friend come into your diner for safety. There must be something that we can do, you know, to repay you. We don't have much money."

"No, no — it'sa fine. There is no-ting for you to'a repay. There are too many crazy people out'a there. You must be careful," he said, in his broken English, as he shook his finger at them.

"Please, we can wash the pots in the kitchen, maybe trade for a small meal?"

Now the old man's suspicions were peaked. He stepped back, took a good hard look at the two girls standing before him and that was when he noticed how dirty they were. There was road dust all over both of them. Their shoes, their legs, and especially their clothing were filthy. He figured that they probably haven't eaten in a long time either.

"You two - no from here, yeah?"

Lee, who suddenly became the brave one, spoke up.

"No, we have been traveling from New York. We are trying to get to New Mexico because our father is dying. We lost most of our money back in Iowa, when we were robbed. We walked most of the way, but sometimes we would get a ride from a nice truck driver."

Appalled by what he was hearing, he called out to his wife.

"Claudia, com'a here quick."

"Why — wha'sa matter Gino?" she said as she sauntered around the corner.

"Look at these two girls. Make som'ting to eat, hurry up too."

Claudia wasted no time and scurried back into the kitchen. Gino then looked at the pair and said,

"Tonight, you com'a home with me and da missus. She gonna wash your clothes, you tak'a da bath and sleep in a real bed. Tomorrow, you eat and then you can head to your papa, with a full belly."

The girls were so happy that they both hugged him — at the same time.

Claudia busied herself in the kitchen cooking up some pasta for the girls. She took some fresh bread that she had made earlier in the day and put it in the oven to warm it up. As she put the pot of sauce on the stove to warm it up, she decided to get some meatballs out of the icebox and throw them into the warming sauce.

As she bustled around the kitchen, she heard the girls giggling and her husband Gino laughing. Oh it felt good to hear happiness and joy come from her Gino again. It had been a long time since she last heard her Gino sound happy, really truly happy.

Claudia and Gino Carozza had two children, a son named Mateo and a daughter named Rosa. Mateo enlisted in the army and was shipped over to Germany to fight in the war. They hadn't heard from him in over three months and every morning Claudia would walk down to the post office, rosary in hand, to check the list of the missing and dead soldiers, praying that her son's name would not be on it.

Rosa, her daughter, had gotten married six years earlier. She begged her not to marry Victor, because he seemed like a mean and brutal man. But, Rosa was so in love with him and there was no chance that either of her parents could talk any sense into her.

Even though Gino and Claudia did not approve, it didn't stop them from giving their only beloved daughter a beautiful wedding. She was the most beautiful bride and as parents, they could not have been prouder of their beloved child. Claudia prayed daily that Victor would be a good husband and a good provider for her daughter. But, not long after they got back from their honeymoon and moved into their new apartment, Victor started hitting her. Claudia begged her daughter to come home, but Rosa wouldn't listen.

One night, Gino had to go over there to break up a fight and that was when he took Victor outside in the backyard. Gino pulled out a gun that he had brought over and showed it to him. He then said,

"Victor, I promise you, you'a lay another finger on my daughter Rosa again, I will com'a back here and I kill you myself."

Victor did not scare easily. He raised one hand, placed it on his father in-law's right shoulder and pushed him out of the way, as he said to him,

"Go home Gino, you are never welcomed here again. And, I'll make sure that Rosa knows the rules too. Now get out of here before I do something that you will regret."

It didn't take long, less than a year later, their beautiful daughter Rosa was dead — Victor had broken her neck. The police were looking for him, but he fled to New York in a hurry. He is still wondering around free — somewhere. Even though the police were still looking for him, and he's a wanted man, he was still out there roaming the streets.

So, as for now, Gino and Claudia were childless. She missed having someone other than her husband to fuss over. At her age, she should have had grandchildren running around and getting into everything. With her beloved daughter dead and her only son in the army, there was no telling if she and Gino would ever be granted the gift of a grandchild.

The thought brought tears to her eyes and that was something that she didn't want Gino or their guests to see. As she grabbed the bottom of her apron to wipe the tears from her face and eyes, she heard footsteps heading her way. Quickly, she turned away so that whoever it was, they would not be able to see her face and find out that she had been crying.

Gino entered the kitchen to find Claudia cooking up some pasta and meatballs for the young girls. He had gone over to the oven to remove the bread that he smelled warming inside of it.

"Claudia, when we finish here and da girls are fed, we gonna bring dem home, to our house."

She quickly turned to look at her husband to see if he was serious — and he was.

"They are'a so dirty,' he pleaded to her, 'and I tella dem that they can a tak'a da bath and sleep in a nice'a warm bed tonight. I know it'sa late and you are tired, but I help'a you to wash'a da clothes."

"Gino — you know nothing about washing da clothes. Nev'a you mind, my sweet, kindhearted husband. I will tak'a care of it."

Joy filled her inside. It had been a long, long time since anyone had slept in the spare room. She looked forward to having company, even if it was only for one night.

As soon as the food was ready, she prepared two generously filled plates, giving the girls two extra meatballs than the usual customers get and brought them out to the dining area. As the girls ate — more like devoured —their food, Gino and Claudia looked on. Claudia took a slice of bread and said,

"You like'a da pasta?"

The girls were too busy shoveling it into their mouths to answer, but to Claudia, that was answer enough and she smiled.

"How long since you'a eat a good meal?" she asked, and that

was when Gino piped up.

"Claudia, basta, stia zitto," he said in Italian, telling her to be quiet. *"Can you see dey are busy? Stop'a and wait 'til they eat first."*

"I'm'a sorry, I wait then," she said as she stuck a piece of bread into her mouth and began to chew.

With their meal consumed and everything cleaned up and ready for tomorrow's business, Gino, Claudia and the two girls headed home. Once they got inside, the girls sniffed the air. The house had a wonderful smell to it. It was a home that had plenty of fine meals prepared in it —meals that required lots of garlic. They removed their shoes at the door and lickety-split, Claudia zipped down the hall to start gathering up something for the girls to slip into while she washed their clothes.

"Gino, get two towels and show the girls where the washroom is, they need da bath." She returned with some night shirts for the girls and said,

"You two put deeze on'a for bed and give'a me your clothes, I gonna wash'a dem tonight."

While one bathed, the other kept company with their hosts, the Carozza's. Each explained that they were trying to get to New Mexico to help their sick — and possibly dying — father. Both girls kept most of the bad stuff that happened to them out of their stories, as well as keeping the Carozza's suspicions at bay. Claudia showed the girls to the guest bedroom and soon the lights were out for the night.

Lee tossed and turned most of the night, but Lucy slept like a rock. When morning came, the girls had decided that they wanted to do something nice for the wonderful couple that took them in. They headed to the kitchen to prepare a breakfast for their rescuers, but Claudia was already cooking and Gino was squeezing fresh oranges — enough for everyone.

"Bon journo" Gino said. *"You sleep'a good?"*

Standing side by side, the girls said in unison,

"Yes, thank you."

"We were going to make breakfast for the two of you, you know, to thank you for all that you have done for us." Lucy said.

"Ah, nev'a you mind," Claudia said. *"You'a sit down and eat'a your breakfast now. When you done, your clothes are hanging on'a da line and you can'a get dressed."*

After the girls finished eating, they took their plates to the sink and started cleaning up the mess. Claudia tried, unsuccessfully, to get them to stop. The two, zipped around the kitchen with precise direction, just like they did back in the coffee shop in Ohio. In less than fifteen minutes, the Carozza's kitchen was spotless.

While the girls were dressing, Lee asked Lucy,

"What do you think about asking the Carozza's if we could stay on for a week? We could work in the restaurant and earn a few dollars each and then we can go on our way."

Lucy thought about it and agreed. Staying with these nice folks would be good — if they would have them. Besides, they were tired of being on the road. They were tired of sleeping in the fields, or looking for a safe place to hunker down.

They pitched their idea of staying on for a while, to the Carozza's and without as much as a moment's delay, Gino accepted their offer. Claudia too, was happy to have the girls stay. It wasn't long before the week came and went. The girls stayed on for an extra two weeks. Finally, the time came for them to start their travels again. This time though, they had enough money to buy a train ticket.

Gino and Claudia packed them a bag with some food and they even bought the girls good winter coats. Even though it was still typically warm out, for late September, the nights were starting to get cold and they just didn't want to think about the girls being out there with not enough protection from the elements.

The girls were extremely grateful for everything that the Carozza's had given them, and asked for their address so that they could send them postcards along the way. This way they could let them know how they were doing and where they were.

Gino and Claudia brought the girls to the train station and waited until they boarded before they left for work. Claudia started crying and that got everyone else crying too. The Carozzas didn't want the girls to leave and according to Lucy, they really didn't want to leave either. But, they had lied to them about their sick and dying father and now they had to stick to their story. How would it look if they chose to stay on and not even bother to check in on their dying dad? So, having no choice and not wanting to be found out — they had to leave.

After everyone exchanged hugs and kisses, the girls boarded the train — legally this time. As the train rolled down the tracks, away from the station, the girls plastered themselves against the window, waving to the Carozza's until they were no longer in view.

I believe Lucy told me that they became pen pals for quite a long time, well at least until their deaths. She said that she even traveled back for Gino's funeral and stayed with Claudia for a week or so to help her get through it. Lucy also learned that, not long after she and Lee left for New Mexico, Gino and Claudia received a letter from the government. It was notification stating that that their son Mateo, died in action. Isn't that terrible?

CHAPTER 12

Settling down into their seats, the girls chatted softly to each other about their excitement of actually getting to New Mexico. They talked about each stop along their route and began making plans as to what they were going to see and where they were going to go. They talked for hours when Lee noticed that one of the passengers, a strange looking man, was paying a bit too much attention to them. He was sitting a few rows ahead of them, but he kept turning around and looking their way. Quietly, she got Lucy's attention and said,

"I'll get up and go to the bathroom. Maybe I can get a better look at him as I pass by, then we'll know if we need to worry or not."

"OK."

Lee got up, slowly walked down the aisle and headed for the bathroom. The man watched her go by, but he never moved. When she got back, the two girls figured that he was just a harmless creepy old man. Going about their business and not paying attention to him or too much to anything else either, they eventually fell asleep, listening to the rhythm of train gliding along the track."

Glancing down at her watch again, Kari noticed that it was getting late and that it would probably be a good idea to get Tess back into the building.

"I think we have to put the story on pause for a while Tess, we have been out here for quite a while and I think we ought to check-in."

Looking at Tess's face, Kari could tell that she was not happy with her decision. Unless she was willing to communicate her objections verbally, Tess had no choice but to wait for the rest of the story.

Kari wheeled her back to the building and into her room. Once inside, she asked her if she needed any help getting out of the chair or into the bathroom. Tess allowed Kari to assist her to a standing position, but that was all. She got hold of her walker and made the rest of her journey to the bathroom — on her own.

Dinner was delivered promptly at six and as Tess started eating; Kari mentioned that she had something wonderful planned for the next day and they were going to have a great day outside. For a brief moment, Tess paused and straightened her back, signaling that she was not ok with the new arrangement. The problem was, however, Kari had no knowledge of Tess's signals. And even if she did, she wasn't going to let it change her plans.

After dinner and their nightly tea, Kari told Tess that she would be leaving for the night. She asked if she wanted help getting into bed, but Tess just rocked in her rocker — looking out the window at the nothingness of a view. Reluctantly Kari left the room and headed for the locker-room to change her clothes before she went home. As she rounded the corner, she ran right into Melva and almost knocked her to the ground.

"What the…" Melva said after the head-on collision.

"Oh my," Kari said. "I am so sorry. Are you alright?"

"Yeah, yeah, I'm fine. Good thing I didn't hit the ground. If I would have gotten hurt, you would have a big problem on your hands, missy."

"What problem?" Kari innocently asked.

"What do you mean what problem? Trying to take care of my patients, as well as Miss Parker — kind of problem." Pausing briefly, she then asked,

"Speaking of Miss Parker, where in the devil have you been with her? I haven't seen nor heard from you all day."

Kari gave her the short version of events. She told her about their breakfast together, then lunch and about their walks out in the backyard. She told her that they would sit at the end bench looking at whatever wildlife came around. She really didn't want to bore her with the story telling part nor get into Tess's small improvements that she had been making, in just two days. That was something that could wait — at least until she had to actually report it.

"Are you heading out now?"

"Yes, I was just on my way to change. Did you need me to do something before I left?"

Kari was hoping that the answer was no, because she had plans to go shopping before she went home.

"No, I don't need anything. Go on, get out of here and don't forget to punch out before you leave."

Relieved that her services were no longer required, Kari dashed into the locker-room and quickly changed her clothes.

As she drove back to town, she made a few stops along the way. Gathering up some necessary supplies and equipment, she stowed them in the trunk of her car for the evening. She wondered how she was going to get them into the facility the next morning and not raise anyone's suspicions. She was good at making spontaneous decisions, but the problem with that was, she sucked at thinking ahead about the consequences if her plans happen to go awry. "Baby steps," she told herself, "baby steps."

CHAPTER 13

Kari arrived at home and started cooking a small dinner for herself. She opened up the freezer, pulled out a TV dinner and popped it into the microwave. While that was cooking, she managed to make herself a small, yet desirable salad and prepared the table in her most favorite room — the living room. She turned on the television, put her favorite show on — *Mystery Murders* — and ate her dinner, sitting on the couch.

Something came to mind as she watched her program; she remembered something that Lynnette had told her. Whispering Creek had once been some type of a halfway house. There had to be records of it somewhere. Her interest had peaked and now she was on a mission. If Tess wouldn't speak and tell her what happened, then Kari was going to research her and try to find out on her own. Something inside was pushing her and her love for stories of yesteryear seemed to be a driving force.

With her show now over, she got out her laptop and started looking up any articles about Whispering Creek. She found the same, somewhat boring rendition on just about every page.

'Just like home. Whispering Creek is a warm & friendly environment, with gentle, caring staff members, who are there to assist when needed.'

Kari wasn't too sure about the gentle staff members part yet, but she was willing to stick around to find out. After all, she had seen worse places and she knew what signs to look for.

Hours had gone by and she was no further ahead with her investigation than she had been when she started.

"I must be really tired. I can't even think straight," she said to herself. Closing the screen of her laptop, she turned off the television and headed off to bed. As she pulled the covers back, preparing to get in, she realized she was exhausted. She longed to curl up in her warm comfortable bed and fall into a long deep sleep. Being so worn out, she felt that the minute her head touched the pillow, she would be out like a light. But after thirty minutes of tossing and turning, she found herself still wide-awake. Her mind kept traveling back to Tess.

"Why would she have been placed in a halfway house? Why would she never leave — even when she could have?"

Kari's mind was reeling. That was when another idea came to her mind,

"There must be records left in the old part of the building — somewhere."

At least there was some progress in the right direction. Kari had planned on going in to work a little earlier in the morning and have a look around. Of course, she first has to get her supplies out of her trunk and into the facility. Having all that busy work on her mind, she managed to fall into a deep comfortable sleep.

CHAPTER 14

Arriving at the retirement home an hour before her scheduled time, Kari opened the trunk of her car and began unloading the supplies. It took her about twenty minutes to get everything out and transported to the area that it will be needed.

After surveying the grounds, she was happy to find that no one was around. Even the night shift seemed to be non-existent and that was more than she could have hoped for. At least for now, she hoped she would be able to snoop around and not be noticed. One nice thing about the night shift, there are only half the amount of staff members than the day shift and fewer workers on the floor meant there was less of a chance of her being caught.

Kari entered through the front door and quickly slipped down the east hall that led to the laundry room. As she walked down the hallway, she tried to see what was in each room that she passed. She mostly encountered locked doors and all the windows were covered. She expected that. After all, this end of the facility was rarely, if ever, used.

As she searched for the stairway to the basement, Kari quietly followed the long winding hallway and with each advancing step, doubt began to set in. A feeling of uncertainty settled over her as she progressed down the hall and with each step that she took, the realization of her finding the basement entrance down this particular hall began to diminish. Eventually the hallway ran out and her journey had ended — without finding the stairway to the basement.

It must be down a different hall, she thought.

Her failed attempt at finding the basement has now made her more determined than before. Suddenly, an uncontrollable urge began welling up deep inside her, she needed to find any information she could about Tess, and this place. Glancing down at her watch, she found that she still had thirty minutes before she needed to report in so she decided to try another hallway. Turning around, she picked up her pace and headed back towards the main entrance. This time, she was going to take the hallway to the west and see where that would lead.

As she rounded the final corner that lead her back to the front lobby, her pace slowed when she heard some noise coming from the front. They were sounds of shuffling papers, drawers opening and closing, then the familiar sound of a chair rolling across the floor. As she came to the end of the hallway, she stopped. She hoped that she would be able to peek around the corner and see who was in the lobby before they see her. Cautiously, she poked her head out and her eyes fell upon Veeona, who was getting her area set up for the day.

"Great, now what am I going to do?" Kari asked herself. Looking at her watch again, she now had twenty minutes left before her shift started. Taking a deep breath, she walked out into the lobby. Thankfully, Veeona had her back turned and didn't even notice Kari coming in. Quick on her feet, Kari made a fast break for the front door. As she opened it, she turned to face Veeona and made it appear that she was just walking in for the day.

"Good morning Veeona" she said as she gingerly sauntered into the room.

Veeona turned and gave her a smile and greeted her back.

"Good mornin' child. How are you today?"

"I'm great. How are you this fine morning?"

"Well, I wish I was as great as you sound, but at my age, I'm just lucky that this morning I woke to see the sun rise for another day." She said with a chuckle.

"Awe Veeona, you are just too hard on yourself. It is a glorious morning and it is going to turn into a wonderful day. Enjoy every moment of it because who knows how many more any of us have."

"You got that right, honey. Like I said before, at my age, seeing the sun rise each morning is a blessing and I know it."

Veeona had busied herself at her desk, finishing getting her things in order, when Kari asked her a straight question.

"Veeona — how long have you worked here?"

"Long time Miss Kari, going on thirty years this July. Why you ask'n? After two days of work'n you already looking to retire?" she laughed.

Kari chuckled and said,

"No, no. It's just that I'd like to know more about this place and I figured, who better to ask than the person who's worked here for a long time. And that Veeona, would be you. So, I was thinking, maybe you'd like to share some of your knowledge of the place with me. What do you think?"

Veeona stopped what she was doing and looked straight at her.

"Now what could you possibly want to know 'bout this old place?" she asked.

"There is so much history here and a bit of a mystery too, don't you think? I just want to know as much as I can. I love to hear about the past."

Pausing just enough to check out Veeona's reaction and hoping that she didn't stir her up in the wrong way, she shot out,

"Hey, what do you think about grabbing some dinner with me after work today? My treat."

Veeona thought about it for a few minutes, then said,

"Why not, it ain't like I got anywheres to be after work and it'd be nice to have dinner with someone, other than myself for a change. OK Miss Kari, it's a date then. Meet you in the parking lot after work."

Kari was elated. "Great! Meet you after work." She started to walk away when, she added,

"Oh, one more thing Veeona, does this building have a basement?"

Veeona, who had already turned her attention back to her morning ritual of moving things around her desk, answered without even a moment of hesitation.

"Sure it does, but nothings down there except for spiders and some dusty old furniture. Why you ask'n?"

"Oh, I was just wondering. Thanks and I'll see you tonight."

Kari headed off to the locker room to change into her scrubs and begin her daily tasks.

CHAPTER 15

Upon entering the room, Kari found that her charge had not only had her breakfast, she was also completely dressed. Expecting to find her seated in her rocker by the window, Kari was even further surprised when she has seen that Tess was sitting in her wheelchair, waiting to be taken outside.

"Good morning Tess, I see that you are ready for this morning's walk. I guess it's a good thing that I brought in our tea already huh?"

Tess held out her hands to take the cups from her, as Kari readily handed them over.

"I have a nice surprise for you today, but first, I have a present for you."

Kari stepped out the door and grabbed a bag that she had placed there earlier. Opening the bag, she pulled out a beautiful white sun hat and presented it to Tess.

"This, my lovely lady, is for you. Now, when we are outside in the sun; you won't get a sunburn on your face. Do you mind if I put it on you?"

She had seen that Tess's eyes had softened, signaling to her that she didn't mind at all. Kari approached her and gently placed the hat on top of her head.

"Oh, it is perfect for you Tess. It looks absolutely beautiful on you."

Kari grabbed a small mirror off the dresser and held it up so Tess could see what she looked like in the hat. Looking at herself in the mirror, Kari knew deep within her soul, that Tess approved. Then, as to confirm her suspicions, Kari saw a big smile in Tess's reflection in the mirror.

"Before your hands tire from holding onto those cups, I better get us outside."

Grabbing the handles of the wheelchair, Kari headed out to the yard. When she stopped at the patio table, thinking that they would sit there while drinking their tea, Kari noticed that Tess had another idea. Instead of setting the tea down, she held firm and turned her head to face the pathway to her now favorite bench.

"Oh you want to sit down there already? OK, hang on to the cups." Kari said, as she pushed her down the path.

"Once we are done with our tea Tess, I have a wonderful surprise in store for you. I hope you'll like it."

Kari's statement was met only by silence, as usual. Nevertheless, she hoped that in the coming days, that might change.

"Well, while we are sitting here, I might as well finally finish Lucy's story. I didn't think it would take this long to get it out. All right, let's begin. Where did I leave off?"

Getting herself situated and making sure that Tess was in a comfortable position, she began, once again, to take Tess on the journey through Lucy's life story.

"They were sleeping on the train that was taking them to New Mexico when they felt the train jerking and heard the screeching of the wheels bringing the train to a stop. They woke to find that the train was pulling into a small depot, but they had no idea where they were. The conductor had come through the car and told them that they will be stopping for a few hours while they refill the train's water tank. Everyone was welcomed to get off the train and visit the town, but they had to make sure that they were back before the train left the station.

The girls decided to get off the train and explore the town. Besides, they needed to stretch their legs for a bit. What they didn't seem to notice was that, the creepy old guy that was sitting ahead of them, also got off the train and began to follow them.

It didn't take them long to find out that they were in Kansas, some little town called, Litchfield. Normally the girls always stayed together, but this time they split up and went their own way to explore the town. Lucy wanted to go window-shopping and Lee wanted to stop in at the soda shop and have a milkshake.

Before they left Nebraska and the Carozza's, Gino had made sure that both girls had enough money for their trip. So, for the first time since Lee left home, she was able to buy something that she really wanted and right now, what she wanted was a milkshake.

While Lee was in the soda shop, Lucy walked down the sidewalk looking in the windows of all the wonderful little shops that ran up and down Main Street. She had been so engrossed in seeing all the little treasures in the shop windows that, she didn't even notice the creepy guy from the train had slipped between the buildings into the alley.

Lucy made her way down the street on one side, crossed the street and walked all the way back up the other side. As she crossed the street to get over to the soda shop to meet up with Lee, she thought she heard a cry for help. Not sure which way the sound had come from, she quickened her pace and went back down the sidewalk, where she originally started. As she passed the soda shop, she hastily peeked in the window and realized that her friend was no longer inside. Then, she heard the sound of a scuffle.

The noise was coming from further down the way and she quickly headed towards it. As she came to the entrance of the alley, between the two buildings, she prepared herself for what she might see, but what she saw when she peered into the alley was — absolutely nothing. She was just about to leave when, she heard loud a cry. Looking at the ground around her, searching for some sort of weapon, she found a broken piece of lumber. Grabbing it, she courageously headed down the alley.

Lucy carefully and quietly crept down the alley. She had gone three quarters of the way to the end when she was met with a pile of boxes and a bunch of smelly garbage. As she searched the immediate area, she found Lee lying on the ground. There was blood coming from her lip, her right eye was bruised and swollen and the creepy guy from the train was on top of her — raping her.

Lucy only needed a second to make sense of what was happening. She immediately raised the piece of lumber as if it were a baseball bat and she swung it with all her might. She hit him on the upper shoulder, near his right ear. He was just about ready to release his nasty jizum in her, when he received the hit. Stunned, he pulled out and with his privates hanging in the open, Lucy raised her weapon again and this time she connected with his head.

He hit the ground hard and didn't move. Lucy yelled at Lee to get up and run.

As Lee ran to the other end of the alley, Lucy kicked the guy. First she kicked him in the face and then in his exposed privates. She hoped she caused enough damage to his pecker that the next time he tried to have sex; he wouldn't be able to get it up.

Lucy took Lee back to the soda shop and headed straight to the bathroom, to help clean her up.

"Are you alright Lee? How did this happen?"

"I don't know Lucy. I was at the soda shop, having a milkshake and that creepy guy from the train came in. He sat down next to me and ordered a coffee. I started to get the heebie-jeebies so, I decided to leave and come find you."

She stopped while she blew her nose and wiped away the blood that was running out, as Lucy gently wiped the tears from her face.

"I got as far as the alley when, he charged at me. He pushed me behind the boxes and he had his hand over my mouth and.... and... You know the rest," she sobbed.

Lee wasn't able to bring herself to even mouth the words of what that horrible, disgusting man did to her. All Lucy could do was, wrap her arms around her poor wounded friend, and hug her as tightly as she could.

With Lee's wounds cleaned up as much as they could be, the girls decided to head back to the train. On their way back, Lucy stopped at one of the local stores and bought a hat with a nice wide brim so that Lee could hide her bruised face, at least until it healed.

"Oh, Lucy, thank you. I love it."

"It looks good on you too, Lee. Even with a shiner, you are still beautiful. You are going to make a great movie star, when we finally get to Hollywood, that is."

"When we get there and if things go the way we plan, you won't have to worry about a thing. I'll make enough money to take care of both of us, for the rest of our lives."

"I'll hold you to it Lee, be careful what you say now."

"I mean it Lucy, I owe you my life."

The girls made it back on the train and as it was starting to roll down the tracks, they both sighed with a breath of relief when the creepy guy two rows up, wasn't in his seat.

"Guess Mr. Creepy decided he liked the view in Litchfield and chose to stay in town," Lucy said.

"Do you think he's still alive? You hit him pretty hard Lu, he had blood coming out of his ear you know."

"Well, if he's dead, too bad. He deserved it." Lucy's words were cold and full of malice. She didn't realize how much anger she still had pent up inside her until she had seen that guy on top of her friend. It brought back the memory of her own rape, back when she first left home. She remembered all too clearly, that sickening smell of his fluids as he thrust himself back and forth, inside her. How his hot breath hit her face, as he breathed heavily into it. The mere thought of it made her sick to her stomach, all over again.

"What's the matter Lucy? You look lost in your thoughts."

Lucy never told anyone that she was raped and even though she and Lee had shared the same horrible nightmare, Lucy couldn't open up to her — at least not yet.

"It's nothing. Don't worry about me. What did that guy say to you back in the alley?" she asked.

Nervously, Lee responded

"Nothing. He was too busy ripping off my panties and sticking his thing inside me. Oh, I think I'm going to throw up Lucy. I don't want to think about it."

"Well you have to Lee — you have to remember, because he just may come back. So let's have it. He said something to you. I heard him talking. I just couldn't make out the words."

Pausing for a moment, Kari broke from her story and said,

"I believe that Lee finally told Lucy what the guy said, but she never told me. I also believe there was a lot of the story that Lucy left out too. I'm not sure why, but every time I tried to push her for more information, she would just clam up for the rest of the day.

Anyway, the train had made several more stops and that was where it started to get a little foggy. Lucy had cut a big chunk of the story out by telling me it was all just boring stuff.

Eventually the train stopped in New Mexico, where they both

got off. It was a beautiful medium size town and with the girls now short on money, they decided to stay on for a while. Both girls had found a job at the local diner and that was where Lucy met her future husband, Charles.

It took a month for them to save enough money for one train ticket to Hollywood. Lucy was more than happy to give up her share of earnings to Lee, so that she could buy a ticket. Lucy decided she was going to stay in New Mexico because Charles had just proposed to her.

"Lee, I know you don't have to be in California by any special date and I'd like to ask if you wouldn't mind waiting another week before you go."

Feeling hurt that her best friend had just bailed on her, Lee was hoping against hope that Lucy just might change her mind about staying.

"What do you mean — wait another week? For what?"

"I'd like you to be my Maid of Honor. I don't have anyone except you and besides, everything that we have been through together makes you my best friend — forever."

Happily surprised, Lee said, *"Of course I'll be your maid of honor. I'm so happy for you Lucy. Maybe when I get married, you can come and be in mine too."*

"Well, even if I'm not your maid of honor, you better at least invite me to the wedding." They hugged each other as they both began to laugh.

The wedding was a beautiful event and the happy bride was absolutely gorgeous. Lee ended up leaving for California the day after the wedding, as the newlyweds headed off to the groom's family cottage for their honeymoon. Over the years, Lucy ended up having a couple of children, but I've never seen any of them. In the three years that she was at Shepherd Gate, I was her only visitor.

She claimed that she had kept in contact with Lee for years. Then like everyone else, she too seemed to fade away. I never looked her up to see if she ever made it in Hollywood and if she had made something of herself. She probably changed her name or something. It would be nice to know what ended up happening to her, right?"

Pausing, Kari glanced down to the pavement as she felt a lump coming into her throat. She couldn't believe that she had an urge to cry. Swallowing hard, she hoped the lump would subside and eventually it did — some. Then she continued.

"On the day that Lucy died, she asked me to put her makeup on and fix her hair. She handed me a picture of herself and told me to make her look just like she did in that photo. That day, we had a marvelous time as I did her hair and put on her makeup. We talked and laughed through it all. In the evening, after I got her settled into her bed just before I left for the night, she asked me to sit with her. I climbed into her bed, sitting right next to her and held her in my arms. She held onto my hand and said something that I didn't understand.

"Kari" she said, *"I promised to take my secret to my grave and as much as it pains me to keep this secret — a promise is a promise."*

I had no idea what she was talking about, but I figured that she wanted to clear her conscience or something. She leaned over, kissed my cheek and as soon as she settled back into her pillow, she took her last breath. It wasn't long after her passing that I decided to quit working there. I took all my vacation time, a whole month's worth and moved over to here. At least one good thing came out of that stupid place though, since Lucy didn't have any relatives to claim her, the facility gave me all her possessions and in turn, they allowed me the privilege to give her a nice little funeral. It was small, but I'm sure she would have approved."

Kari sat quietly for several minutes, waiting for the feeling of sadness to whisper away. Tess too looked sad and if Kari wasn't mistaken, she thought she saw a tear swelling in Tess's eyes.

Feeling that she was bringing down the mood, she rose from the bench, took Tess's empty cup to discard it as she said,

"Are you ready for your next surprise Tess? I know Lucy's story was a long one and it seemed like there should be more. I couldn't agree with you more on that, but that was all I could get out of her and believe me, I tried."

Grabbing the handles of the wheelchair, Kari started to push Tess away from the bench area. However, instead of staying on the path, Kari pushed her through an opening between the trees and out onto the grassy lawn. As they approached, what used to be a flower garden, Kari's supplies came into full view.

CHAPTER 16

What used to be a flower garden was now just a huge pile of weeds. Some of the perennials, planted forever ago, were still trying to bloom. However, with all the weeds choking their roots and no one to tend to them, they pretty much just went wild.

As they arrived at the flowerbed, Kari positioned the wheelchair near a small tree. It wasn't much, but it would offer some shade from the hot morning sun. Kari then went over to the pile of supplies she had purchased and brought out earlier that morning and grabbed the blanket she had neatly packed. Shaking out the blanket, she spread it out over an area of the lawn closest to the garden, then turned to Tess and asked,

"Tess, how do you feel about helping me whip this weed garden back into its glory days of a flower garden? I have all the stuff that we need to get started at least. If you don't feel like helping, that's fine too, at least you can keep me company. Would you like to come and sit on the blanket?"

Tess had already gotten out of the wheelchair and was walking towards her. Kari helped her as she sat down on the ground. Once she was safely seated, she then proceeded to show Tess all of the things that she had brought out to their project area.

"See Tess, I got two of everything. I have; gloves, small hand shovels, weed pullers, hand tines, buckets for the junk and I even brought some yard waste bags. I also bought two foam kneeling pads so we won't hurt our knees on the rock hard dirt. Once we clear out all this mess and add some fresh dirt, I'll pick up some flowers that we can plant. What do you think? Doesn't this sound like fun?"

Tess's eyes scanned over the supplies and then grabbed a small hand shovel and a pair of gloves. Kari handed her a foam kneeling pad and soon the two were digging in the dirt and pulling out weeds — together.

Kari chatted on endlessly as they worked and of course she was the only one doing all the talking, but she didn't mind. This time, she kept an eye on the time because she didn't want Tess to miss having her lunch. Kari knew how fast time can slip by without even knowing it, especially if the mind is engrossed in something else.

After working in the weed pile for about an hour, Kari sat back, removed her gloves and said,

"Tess, I think we should get back so we can get you cleaned up for lunch."

Tess only continued to pull weeds, ignoring Kari as best as she could.

"Did you hear me, Tess? It's getting late, we should pack it up for today. I don't want you to miss lunch."

Still getting no reaction, Tess just kept turning the dirt with her hand shovel, pulling the gnarled roots out and throwing them in her waste bucket. As Kari started to pack up her tools, the sight of Melva approaching surprised her. She saw her walking across the lawn, headed their way carrying a tray of what looked like food and drinks.

"Well, well, well, what do we have here?" Melva asked.

A little nervous about getting into trouble, Kari carefully responded.

"Oh, hi Melva, Tess and I have been looking at this poor dilapidated ruin of a flower garden and thought that we could breathe some life back into it. Besides, I thought it would be good for Tess to get out more and be a little more active."

Melva, still holding the tray of food that she had brought out to them, looked down at Tess. She had seen that, indeed, the old woman who had become a fixture at the home for so many years, finally started to do something constructive.

"Kari, I think that is a wonderful idea and when I had seen you two working out here through Lola's window — *(Lola was one of Melva's charges)* — I thought that you might like to have your lunches out here on the lawn. I also brought out two bottles of water for the two of you." Noticing the hat, Melva turned towards Tess and said,

"Miss Parker, what a beautiful hat you have, and you look absolutely wonderful in it too. Now y'all be careful of the sun, it may only be the middle of May but, that sun still gets hot."

Handing Kari the tray of food, she turned and said,

"And Kari, don't keep her out here too long. She should come in and maybe take a nap before dinner. You don't want to overexert her on the first day."

"Good point Melva, thanks for the tip."

Melva left the two alone as Kari set the tray out on the blanket.

"Tess, would you prefer to sit in your chair and eat or would you like to sit on the blanket with me?"

Tess, who had been kneeling on the foam pad, pulled off her gloves, dropped them in the dirt and crawled over to the blanket to sit with Kari for lunch. Kari continued to be amazed by Tess, the woman hasn't spoken a word in over twenty-five years yet, with her actions she spoke volumes.

The two women sat in the center of the blanket across from each other and began eating their picnic lunch that Melva had brought out to them. They had chicken salad sandwiches, potato chips, fresh cut fruit, and a piece of banana cream pie. As Kari finished her sandwich, she surveyed all the rest of the food and noticed that Tess was not particularly interested in eating anything other than her sandwich.

"Tess, I think we have a lot of food here and I don't think neither one of us are going to finish it. How about we wrap it up and in about another hour or so we have it for a snack? And, just so you know Tess, I brought a cooler filled with water for us too. I guess Melva couldn't see it through Lola's window. I'll just put our fruit, the pies and the extra water bottles inside so they stay fresh. We can have them in a bit."

After finishing her sandwich, Tess crawled back to the foam pad to continue her weed pulling while Kari cleaned up their lunch mess off the blanket. They continued to work out there for another hour or so and as Kari was fighting with a large root, she felt a soft touch on her shoulder. Looking up, she found Tess standing over her and handing her a bottle of water. Taking it from her, she said,

"Thank you Tess. I'm sorry. I guess I got a little carried away with my work that it slipped my mind to see if you needed anything. Shall we stop for a break and have our fruit or pie?"

Tess took a step to the side so that Kari could see the blanket behind her. She had already taken out the fruit and placed it on the blanket for them to eat it.

"Oh, how wonderful Tess. Alright, let's take a break."

The two women sat in the sun, eating their fruit and from a distance, if one didn't know better, it looked like they were having the most wonderful conversation. But in reality, only one of them was conversing and that was Kari.

CHAPTER 17

Kari brought Tess back into her room around four thirty. This would give her plenty of time to wash up, change her clothes, and take roughly a thirty-minute nap before dinner.

After cleaning up from their first day of yard work, Tess decided to put on her nightclothes, which signaled to Kari that she had enough for one day. Sitting on the edge of her bed, Tess just stared at Kari. Not sure what her charge wanted; Kari went over at sat down on the edge of the bed next to her.

"What's the matter Tess?"

Knowing that she wasn't going to get an answer, her mind started racing. She wanted to try to figure out how to ask a question that Tess could answer.

"Are you tired? Did I keep you out too long? Maybe we can take tomorrow off. It's not like we have a deadline of getting all this done, you know."

Tess looked down and for a brief moment Kari thought Tess was actually going to speak. In the end, what emerged from Tess's mouth was — nothing. Nothing but her usual silence.

Kari rose from the bed and as she stood, Tess took hold of her hand and gave it a gentle squeeze. Looking down at her charge and with a tear in her eye, she said,

"Thank you Tess. Thank you. That means the world to me."

She bent down and gently kissed the top of her forehead before she left the room.

In the locker room, Kari was about to turn on the lights but decided against it. She found a quiet, dark spot in the corner of the room where she sat in the dark. In the silence of the room, she recalled Tess's warm gesture of her holding her hand. It was at that point when Kari realized, that in just three short days, she had become completely and totally captivated with her charge. She was finding that even after losing Lucy, there was still room in her heart for Tess. Her heart had melted when Tess took her hand. She had to bite her tongue, in order to stop the tears from falling, while she stood in front of her. The joy that filled her inside was enormous, as if she would explode — just like an overfilled helium balloon, ready to pop. As her mind replayed that unambiguous moment, over and over again, Kari finally allowed her tears to spill over and roll down her cheeks.

When the tears finally stopped flowing, her feelings of sadness gave way to a simple serene kind of happiness. For Kari, crying had a way of cleansing the soul, giving her a new sense of being. She knew deep within her heart that she and Tess were bonding. Now, more than ever, her determination to find out what happened to her had just become a priority.

Seeing that it was past dinner hour, she jumped up to check on her charge. She made a mad dash down the hallway and when she got to Tess's room, she found the door to 237 ajar. Ever so gently, she pushed open the door and found that, not only did Tess finish eating her dinner; she was tucked in bed and already fast asleep. After picking up the empty dinner tray, she quietly closed the door behind her.

'I must have really tuckered her out today' she thought, *'guess tomorrow we should probably do something different.'*

Realizing it was quitting time, Kari rushed back over to the locker room and changed back to her street clothes.

Entering the parking lot, Kari heard someone call out her name.

"Kari — Kari, over here."

Turning towards the voice, she had seen who was calling out her name.

"Oh, hi Veeona" she called back.

"Kari, are we still on for dinner tonight?"

She had completely forgotten about the dinner plans that she had made earlier that morning. After all that happened with Tess today, Kari had let everything slip from her mind.

"Of course we are Vee. Where do you want to meet? I can follow you, if you'd like."

"That would be great. I know a really nice little place just down the road."

They each got into their own cars, where Kari followed Veeona to a little diner called, The Dirty Duck.

CHAPTER 18

As Kari was parking her car, she peered through the windshield at the restaurant that Veeona had led her to. A dingy little hole in the wall that gave her the creeps — the name didn't help it any either. Slowly she opened her car door, a little unsure if she really wanted to go inside, then she heard,

"Are you getting out or what?"

Standing at the back of her car was, Veeona.

"Are you sure this is a safe place Vee? I mean, look at it."

Kari was very uneasy about going inside, let alone eating the food.

"Awe kid com'on, don't let the name or the outside of this ol' place fool ya. This is a gem in the rough," she told her.

"I'll say, *rough* is a great word to describe this place," she said, as she let out a forced pretend chuckle.

"Wait till you're inside and you taste the food. But, you got to be quick."

"Why? What will happen?"

"Well, if ya ain't quick at eatin', the roaches are liable to carry off with your meal."

Veeona couldn't keep a straight face for long, even if she was handed a million dollars. Seeing the look on Kari's face was priceless.

"Veeona, you keep it up and I won't go in there at all and you will be eating fast food this evening."

"Awe, I's just messing with ya sugar. No harm done. Com'on, let's get inside."

They entered The Dirty Duck and Kari was absolutely flabbergasted. As soon as she stepped inside, her feet refused to move. It was as if they were submerged into a pool of deep, thick mud. Grabbing onto Veeona's arm and giving her a slight gentle squeeze, she let out a small quiet gasp. The inside was truly a gem.

"See, I told ya it was nice."

Smiling and shaking her head, Veeona headed to her favorite table as Kari slowly followed behind her, while her eyes were scanning everything in and around the room.

The restaurant was beautifully decorated and there were at least a dozen tables in the dining area. Some of the tables were square and some were round, but all of them were covered in clean white table linens. Adorning each table was a fresh, yet exotic centerpiece. A simple glass vase, half filled with water that had floating candles in them. The warm glow of the candlelight added a romantic nuance to room. On the side of each vase were two narrow glass tubes, which held real fresh foliage. Something unique that Kari had never seen before.

There was recessed lighting and three beautiful chandeliers that hung from the ceiling. The décor resembled an exquisite, and expensive French Bistro in Paris.

The walls, painted bright white, were fashioned with gold tone crown molding throughout. Gold tone appliqués along the ceiling embellished the accents beautifully. Large beautiful landscape paintings, strategically placed, had adorned one side of the room while long white curtains, draped the two narrow arched windows that were on the back wall.

As soon as the two women were seated, their server approached, seemingly out of thin air. Kari was a little startled when she heard,

"Well hi Veeona, today isn't Friday. What brings you in today?"

"Hi Marla, I's just thought to bring my friend Kari here, cuz she's nev'a been here before."

Marla turned and smiled at Kari as she handed them both a menu, then said,

"Well hi there sweetie pie and welcome to the Dirty Duck."

Smiling back, Kari thanked her as she took the menu.

"I'll give you a few minutes to look it over while I get you something to drink. What would the two of you like?"

Veeona said, "We'll both have a coffee Marla, and two tall glasses of ice water, thanks."

Nodding, Marla then headed off to retrieve their drinks.

Not knowing what to expect, Kari opened the menu and her eyes immediately drifted to the price list. Seeing the dinners were of reasonable rates, she then allowed herself to read the description of each of the meals.

"Have ya decided what y'all want to order Kari?" Veeona asked.

"No, not yet. I just can't believe this place or the menu," she said. "There are so many choices that I can't make up my mind as to what my stomach is craving for."

"Well, ya better make up your mind soon, cuz when she gets back here you bes' be ready."

"Alright, just give me another minute then."

As Kari was diligently going over the menu, Veeona pulled out her compact mirror from her purse. First checking her hair, then she got up close and personal to the mirror in order to dig something out of her eye. When she finished messing with her eye, she lowered the mirror down to her mouth and checked her teeth, making sure that nothing was stuck in between them.

As Marla came back towards the table carrying two cups of coffee, Veeona closed her mirror, and as she was putting it away, as she said,

"Time's up sugar, Marla's on her way back."

"OK, I think I know what I want to try."

Setting the cups down onto the table, Marla then grabbed her pen and order pad.

"Are you two lovely ladies ready to order?"

"Yep" Veeona said. "I'll have the usual."

"One Pot Roast, alright and what would you like sweetie?"

Kari finally tore her eyes away from the menu and said,

"I'll have the lobster stuffed ravioli with a side salad."

"Oh, that's a good choice honey. That is an excellent dish. Is there anything else that I can get for you ladies?"

Both women shook their heads in unison and with that, Marla turned and headed to the kitchen to place their orders.

"Vee, how long has this place been here?"

Veeona chuckled and said,

"Oh, the Dirty Duck has been here for years. Although, since its inception, it was a place no better than its name. Old man Ollie opened her up back in '48, I guess. Back then, there was nothing out here, but woods and a large pond. Only hunters used to frequent this place. They hunted deer, the occasional bear, squirrels, but mostly duck — hence the name — The Dirty Duck. Well, when old man Ollie died four years ago, his kin wanted nothing to do with the place, so they put it up for sale.

Rocky Calvert bought the place for his wife Ellen. She had an eye for beauty, as you can see, but that beauty came with a hefty price tag. Poor Rocky, he no sooner got the place fixed up just the way she wanted it and the day after they opened the doors for business — Ellen died."

"Oh no! What happened?"

"Awe, the rumor was, she died in her sleep. Heart attack or something, I don't know for sure. Anyway, Rocky hired Marla right away to help him out. Now she pretty much runs things around here. Some of us regulars think she might be making a move to get into Rocky's bed, if she hasn't already — know what I mean honey?" she said with a shit-eating grin on her face.

Kari was glued to her seat and hanging on every word that Veeona spoke. She wanted to know the whole story. It was then that she remembered why she was there. She had questions of her own that needed answers.

"That is such a sad story Vee. So, how is Rocky doing now?"

"He don't come here much, anymore. Say's it reminds him too much of Ellen. He's still in love with her ya know, and that's gonna be a tough road for Marla to cross, if that's her intensions. But, I give her credit, she's a patient woman — to some degree, that is," she chuckled.

Looking down at her coffee cup, Kari wasn't sure how to bring up what she really wanted to talk about. Oblivious that Veeona was watching her, Kari just stared at the mini whirlpool spinning in her coffee, as she stirred her spoon around and around.

"So Miss Kari, what do you want to know about Whispering Creek that you are being so gracious to buy me dinner for?"

Relieved that the moment was no longer an awkward one, Kari took a sip of her coffee and began with her first question.

"Well Vee, I was curious to find out what you know about the old place. You know, from the beginning."

"Oh that's a tall order honey, we could be here for hours."

"I don't have any plans for the evening — what about you?" she asked with a wink and a smile.

"I ain't got no plans neither, so I guess now's as good a time as any then."

Taking a deep breath, Veeona took a sip of her coffee, then began to tell her tale.

"Alright, let's see. Whispering Creek began in the '80's — 1986 to be exact. Before it was a retirement home, it was a mental asylum, before that, it was a woman's halfway house and before that, it was a woman's prison."

"Really?"

"Yes, really. Now you just hush and let me talk. I'm an old woman and I'm liable to forget what I'm talkin' about, probably in mid-sentence too" she chuckled.

Marla returned with their meals and as the two began to eat, Veeona told her story.

CHAPTER 19

"In the beginning, back in '36, that old building started out a woman's prison. It didn't have many inmates, but there were a few. It operated as a prison from '36 until the first part of '48. The prison was closed down when they found out what the Warden was doing out there. He had been having his way with all those locked up women there, just as if those prisoners were his personal harem. I had heard that some of them inmates didn't mind kickin' boots with him either. My guess is, because having sex probably broke up the monotony of them being cooped up all day long in their tiny cells, I reckon. But, what got all them women upset was — him doing nasty things to the young ones.

The story I was told was this: one day a raging beauty of a young gal in her mid-twenties had been arrested for killing a man that she claimed had raped her. Of course, back then the police weren't as thorough at their investigating as they are now. And what made matters worse, there were no witnesses to the crime. They based their guilty verdict on one stupid fact. She didn't have any ripped or torn clothes on her body. Like that should've made a difference. Nowadays, they have ways to check those poor girls that get raped and the police have a better chance at catching those dirty pigs that do that kind of awful stuff to women.

Anyhow, the Warden had an eye out for that young pretty one ever since the day she walked the line and entered into the prison. The guards checked her in, gave her a shower, her prison uniform, and then escorted to her cell — her new home for a long while.

Well, as the story goes, she had made friends with her cellmates right away. And within three days of her being there, the whole prison yard was out to protect this young pretty thing. Then eventually it happened. It was on the fifth night of her being in the jail when the Warden sent his guards for her.

As they came to collect her, her cellmate somehow managed to convince them that she was sick and to leave her be. Miraculously they did. But the very next night, the warden sent another guard down to collect her. He said that he was under orders to bring her to the warden, no ifs, ands, or buts. This time the cellmate told the guard that the new girl's *'time of the month'* started and once again, the guard left empty handed.

I'm guessing the Warden had an itch'n in his pants that needed to be scratched, so he had the guards bring him three other women in her place. They said that when he was done with those three girls and they brought them back to their cells, those girls should have gotten medical attention. He messed them all up bad. All three had blackened eyes, swollen lips and they were all bleeding down yonder — if you know where I mean." Pointing down to her own crotch area to make sure Kari got the gist of what she was saying.

"I don't know what the hell he did to those women, but that was the beginning of the end for that sick bastard. Those women weren't in that jail cuz they were saints you know. Some were hardened criminals and they wasn't going to just sit there and let that sick SOB of a warden do that to them anymore."

Veeona took a moment to scarf down some food and take a few sips of her coffee before she continued with the story. After all, she figured there was no reason why she should be eating a cold meal when someone else was paying for it. Besides, her throat was getting a little dry from all the talking that she was already doing.

She finished about half her plate of food and polished off her cup of coffee, knowing that Marla would be back shortly to fill it back up. She took a sip of water, feeling it slide down her throat, and then continued where she left off.

"The leader of the inmates was Vie. They appointed her as their leader, mainly cuz she had the most education out of them all. She knew how to read and write, which was probably more than the other girls could do, given the times.

They said that when Vie saw what condition those girls were in when the guards brought them back to their cells — she began writing a letter. She gave it to one of the guards that had a thing for her and asked him to mail it, which he did. The letter was addressed to the governor, she begged him to investigate the prison. She told him everything that the warden was doing out there and described it in very explicit detail. She explained how the warden was abusing the women and how he was cheating the state out of money too.

The next day, the guard that was sweet on Vie, confirmed he mailed her letter. So now, with the letter safely in the hands of the US Postal Service, Vie got the girls together and started organizing a plan. She told all the girls that whenever one of the guards was to show up at their cell, they all had to tell them that it was her time of the month. The regulars — you know, the ones that didn't mind having that sick, dirty pig, put his nasty over sexed penis inside them, offered to go in their place. Finally, he got around to sending for the new girl again. But Vie was gonna make sure that the pig didn't put his filthy hands on her. She requested a special meeting with him instead.

I always thought that if Vie knew the governor was coming out the very next morning, she would have done things differently. But, she had no way of knowing it. Poor Vie, mmm hmmm. Unfortunately for her, Vie had her meetin' with the warden and I guess her plan was to tell him that she was pregnant, and it was his child. She was in the room with him for a very long time they said. And about an hour before sunrise, they finally brought her back to her cell.

That morning around eight o'clock, the governor showed up at the prison. He met with the Warden for about an hour and when their meeting ended, he asked to meet with Vie. Immediately, two guards came running down to her cell to get her. That's when they found her lying in a pool of blood — dead!

After a thorough investigation, they eventually found out that the Warden had personally tried to give Vie an abortion. As it turned out, she wasn't pregnant — she just lied about it so that he wouldn't take the new girl. The dumb fuck didn't know that it was a lie, he was just scared about being found out. I mean, how would it look if any of the prisoners turned up pregnant and they started having babies? Not to mention that them babies all turn out being the Warden's to be exact. Uhmmm that's what I'm talkin' about.

So, that sick, dirty bastard decided to take matters into his own hands. Vie tried to stop him, she even told him that she made it up but he didn't believe her. He ended up sticking a cut up clothes hanger up inside her and tried to get the baby — the baby that didn't even exist — out of her. He had cut her up so badly that by the time the guards dumped her back into her cell, she had just bled to death.

The other inmates learned what Vie was up to when Rita, her cellmate neighbor, told them that Vie gave her a letter that she wrote just before her visit with the warden. Rita had strict orders from Vie to hang on to that letter, no matter what. If something bad happened to her while she was with the Warden, Rita was to make sure that the letter got into the governor's hands — personally — and she did.

It only took two days for the Governor to dismiss the Warden of his duties and bring him up on charges of prostitution, sexual misconduct, tax evasion, tax fraud, embezzlement of state funds and the list went on from there.

The Warden didn't even make it a week on the outside once the news broke. His wife left him, his kids wanted nothing to do with him and many others had issues with him too. They found him near the cemetery, just down the road from here. There he was, sitting behind the wheel of his car, dead as a doornail. Someone had put two bullets in his head, one in his heart and if that wasn't enough to kill him, they left a message by jamming a knife right in his crotch. Uhmmm, somebody sure wanted their pound of flesh from that sorry bastard, and I don't blame them. He had it coming, that's for sure.

The place finally closed down within the year, and it took them every bit of that year to go through all of those inmates records too. What they found in most of those files was, the majority of those women should have been let go years earlier, but that sick horny prick of a warden kept them locked up for his own pleasure.

Once the state was able to sort everything out, there were a handful of women transferred to other prisons, who still had time to serve. But the rest of them, were released immediately. The problem was, most of those women had nowhere left to go. The governor came to the prison to open their cell doors and personally release them when one of the now ex-prisoners, asked if the jail could be converted into a halfway house. She explained how they could take the cell bars off and reorganize it, making it more like a home. I guess it didn't take the governor long to agreed and soon he gave them the money that was needed to convert the place over.

It was reported that the governor himself even rolled up his sleeves to help them get their project started.

As the years went by, the state cut back on the amount of money that they had been sending to the women of the halfway home and soon after, they were no longer able to run the place. So, in the early '60's, the state converted it to an asylum for the insane. It ran until '86. That was about the time when the President of the United States ordered all the states to close state-run institutions and send all those ill patients out onto the streets. Do you remember that? That was a sad day for so many people. Well, not long after that, the Melvin Berkley Group bought the place and turned it into a retirement home."

"Oh my, what happened to all the women then?"

"Well, in case you missed it, Tess was the young girl that Vie was protecting. She didn't want that dirty warden touching her."

"Yeah, I kind of figured that out, but what I want to know is, what happened to Tess while she was in there?"

Veeona shot a quick look across the table at Kari and became a bit suspicious of her question.

"Why does it matter?" Veeona asked.

Feeling a little uncomfortable at the mood change of her dinner companion, Kari chose her words carefully.

"It doesn't matter Vee. I just want to get to know Tess a little better and maybe find out what caused her to stop talking. It's not that I would bring up her past to torment her. I just figured that if I knew more about her, I could deal with her on a different level. Nothing more, nothing less, that's all. Is that OK?"

Veeona let Kari's words sink in for a few moments; she then thought, telling her about Tess's life was not really a big secret after all. All the workers at Whispering Creek know about Tess's past, so why not let her personal caregiver know too.

"Well, alright, I'll tell you what I know. And mind you, I don't know much, as long as you understand that, OK?"

"Understood! Anything you can tell me about her will be more than I know right now."

Veeona took another sip of her coffee, then began telling Kari what she knew about Tess.

CHAPTER 20

"About ten years ago we had a new resident move in, his name was Clarence DuVay. From the day that he moved in, he was under my care. After a few weeks of getting to know each other, I learned that he used to be a guard at the old prison. He loved to tell me stories about his workin' days. But unfortunately, I wasn't real interested in hearing about it. Eventually I figured out that all his talking made him happy. He loved the fact that he had someone, anyone that he could talk to, even if they weren't listening to him.

One day I took him for a stroll out in the yard, just as we had done so many times before. As we were walking, he was looking at the other seniors sitting out in the sun. But on this particular day, he had suddenly started to get choked up and began begging me to get him back inside. Not knowing what was wrong with him, I immediately got him back into his room. I checked him over real good — making sure he wasn't having heart failure or nothin', ya know. I started demanding that he tell me just what in the devil was goin' on."

"What was his problem?" Kari asked.

"His problem was, he'd seen Tess sitting on one of the benches. And after all them years, he recognized her — not that I knew that at the time."

"Oh my. Tell me, was Tess non-verbal already or did she stop talking after that?"

"No, she had already quit talking way before then. In fact, to this day I don't think she even knew that he was there. It took me about a week of coaxing and coddling to get anything out of him. When finally, he spilled the beans. He sang like a canary. In fact, he just wouldn't shut the hell up.

He told me that he had been a guard at the prison for only two years at the time and it sickened him knowing what a pig that warden was. He claimed that even though those women were prisoners, he tried as best as he could to protect them. It sickened him, seeing how they were treated and he didn't believe that any human being should be treated like that — ever. He was mighty glad that the warden got caught when he did and he didn't even shed a tear when he heard that the prick was dead too."

"Why was he so upset when he saw Tess then? I mean, if he didn't do anything to harm her," Kari asked.

"Well now, give me a chance to tell you Kari, it's been so long ago that this happened and I'm trying to remember it as best as I can."

She managed to take a sip of water before she continued,

"Clarence admitted to me, that he was in love with Vie. He was the guard that mailed the letter for her and he was one of the two guards that the governor had picked to retrieve Vie from her cell as well. He was devastated when he found her lifeless body, lying in a pool of her own blood on that nasty cell mattress. And, what was worse, he blamed Tess for it. He figured that if Tess would have just gone in and done her time with the warden, none of this would have happened."

"Are you kidding me? He actually blamed Tess for not taking her turn with that scum bag?"

Kari had completely lost her appetite at that point and pushed her meal away.

"Don't you waste that meal Kari! You ask for a container and eat it later. You'll be glad that you did."

"I doubt it, but alright. Please continue Vee."

"OK, if you think you can handle it."

"I'll be fine — please continue," she said.

"After the Governor left the jail house, Clarence went down to Tess's cell. He said he took her down to solitary confinement — better known as, "the hole". Those cells down there are sound proof you know and I think he wanted to make sure that no noise would travel through the place. I'm guessing that he planned on taking his anger out on her. He told me that he roughed her up a bit at first, but it wasn't until he had stripped her of all her clothes that he came to his senses.

There she was, standing right in front of him, stark naked. All she was wearing was a small trickle of blood that ran down her lip, just staring at him. She wasn't crying. She wasn't begging him to stop. She said nothin' — just stood there like a statue. Staring at him and waiting.

As she stood there in front of him, Clarence took a good hard look at her and something just came over him. He said that she had scars on her body, scars that were in places that scars shouldn't be. Then it hit him. If he was to rape Tess, Vie's death would have been in vain. The woman that he loved so much had died protecting that girl and here he was beating her and planning to rape her himself. All because she didn't take her turn going in to see the warden when it was her turn to be fucked.

He was so ashamed of himself that he grabbed all her clothes, threw them at her as he ordered her to get dressed. When she was done he brought her straight back to her cell. Not a word passed between either of them — the entire time. Once he put her back into her cell, he told me that he headed straight for the time clock, punched out and walked off the job — never to return.

Since he left that job, he said he never got a single night of restful sleep. His every thought was of that old jailhouse and it consumed him; his every waking moment filled with what went on in there and it sickened him.

All these years later, I still think to myself, how ironic it was that in his old age he would show up at Whispering Creek. I wondered why he would come back to the place where the whole damn thing began. Then it became apparent to me. He knew he was dying and after spending all of his life alone, he wanted to die where the love of his life had died. As best as I could tell, I believe his room was next to where Vie's cell would have been — before all the renovations that is. All in all, I think he eventually found his peace, but not until after he had seen Tess."

"What do you mean?"

"After he'd seen her, he stayed in his room day after day. Then one day, when I went into his room, I found him lying in his bed. I thought he was just sleeping, but as I got closer to him, it was evident that he was dead."

Veeona, looked down at the table, pushed her empty plate away and grabbed her cup. For the first time since she began telling her story, she looked sad and her demeanor suddenly became odd. She no longer wanted to continue with the story, but when she looked up and saw that Kari was staring at her, she knew that she was waiting and wanting to hear the end.

"He died in his sleep?" Kari innocently asked.

"Yeah, that's what everyone thought… at first."

Kari was startled when Veeona added the *'at first'* part.

"At first? What do you mean — *'At first'* Vee?"

"I guess I was lucky. After he died, they did an autopsy on him and they found that he had overdosed on his medication. What I didn't know was, that every night when I brought him his pills, he was stashing them instead of taking them. I could have gotten into a whole lot of trouble because I didn't stay and watch him take his meds."

"Oh no! What ended up happening?"

"Good old Clarence left a suicide note and he basically covered my butt when he confessed that he faked taking the meds in front of me. Man-oh-man, I'll tell you; I never ever let that happen again. I watched everyone, from that day forward; I made sure every resident swallowed every pill that I ever gave out. A couple of years later, I transferred to the position that I'm in now — working the front desk."

Veeona sat quietly; sipping her now cold cup of coffee and began to just stared off into the nothingness of space. Kari, who had sat at the edge of her seat the whole time, listening to every word her co-worker spoke, suddenly felt awkward by the silence. Not knowing what to say, she waited for Veeona to make the next move.

It didn't take long before Veeona broke the silence, when she said,

"So, did you get what you wanted Kari? Did you find out all of what you were looking for?"

Taken aback by Veeona's change of tone, she quickly shot a look at her. Fortunately, she saw no malice in her face.

"Vee, first of all, I want to thank you for opening up to me about all this. I now have at least, some idea as to what happened to Tess. I am sorry to hear about your ordeal with Clarence though, and I'm sure that there was nothing that you could have done different to change the outcome of his death."

Looking into Veeona's eyes, Kari could see deep within their depths a cesspool swirling within them that was full of heartbreak.

"Vee, I realize that this all happened years ago and I can see that it troubles you still. If there is anything that I can do to help you get through this and help put this behind you, once and for all, please just let me know."

Veeona smiled at her as she glanced down at her watch. Signaling that it was getting late and it was now time to head on home. Kari thanked her for coming to dinner with her and after she paid the bill, the two moseyed out to the parking lot.

"Vee, I really mean it. If you want me to help you with anything, just let me know."

"Sweetie, those old skeletons don't really scare me much anymore. It's all in the past and I get that. I'm old, my life is coming to the end soon enough, and I know that it's going to be sooner than later. I feel, deep in my heart, that I squared things up with you know who," she said, as she pointed a finger up to the heavens. "And when my time comes to meet my maker, I pray that he will know that I tried my damndest to live my life in the way of the Lord and to follow the Good Book."

Ever so tenderly, Veeona placed her arm around Kari and gave her a little hug. Thanking her again for a wonderful dinner, she then headed for her car. Kari watched her as she walked through the parking lot and get into her car. Soon the engine roared to life and in a blink of an eye; Veeona was on the main road and sped off into the night.

CHAPTER 21

Arriving at home, Kari threw her purse on the couch and grabbed her laptop. She marveled at how much information she had learned from Veeona over dinner this evening. She could barely remember her drive home from the restaurant, due to the wheels spinning in her mind. *"I must have been on autopilot,"* she thought.

Glancing up at the wall clock, she noticed it was too late in the evening for her to start any internet research. Instead, she decided to write down a few notes to help aid her when she did start her research into Tess's history. She was eager to get started, but it would have to wait until tomorrow, after she gets home from work.

Changing into her nightgown, she brushed her teeth and finally slipped between the sheets. As she cozied herself in the bed, she closed her eyes and waited for sleep to wash over her, but the wheels in her mind started spinning again. She rolled onto her side, hoping that the new position would help her drift off to sleep, but that didn't seem to work either. After tossing and turning for about an hour, she gave up and decided to let her mind work a little overtime. While lying there in bed, she started replaying the evening's events in her mind, but slowly and without warning, the inevitable happened — she drifted off to sleep.

With the morning's sunrise peeking through the curtains, Kari's inner alarm clock began to stir her awake. Cautiously she opened her eyes, not wanting the sun to shine directly into them and possibly temporarily blind herself, or at best, get bright spots in her vision. Once her eyes adjusted to the light in the room, she rolled out of bed and headed straight to the kitchen to make herself a much-needed cup of coffee. Then she was off to complete her morning rituals of getting ready for work.

As she walked into the building, she greeted Veeona who was already at her desk, punctual as usual.

"Good morning Vee, how are you this morning?"

"I'm just fine honey, what about you?"

"I'm great and I'd like to thank you for introducing me to the Dirty Duck. Dinner last night, was wonderful."

"Glad you liked it. Maybe we can do it again sometime," Veeona said.

"Oh yes, I'd like that very much. Please let me know when you want to go again."

"Sure will honey, now get a move on before Melva starts docking you for being late. Come on, scoot."

Hustling down the hallway, Kari slipped into the locker room unnoticed. Changing her clothing as quick as possible, she immediately headed straight to Tess's room. As she opened the door, an awesome sight was before her. She found Tess sitting in her wheelchair with her new hat resting comfortably, and quite fashionably, on her head. Somehow, Tess even managed to get a hold of two cups of hot tea, one for each of them. What's more, lying neatly folded over her lap was the picnic blanket, which they had used the day before.

Astounded at the sight, Kari was speechless. Standing there in utter awe of all that Tess had done, Kari lifted her eyes to meet Tess's and it took all of her will power to keep her tears from flowing out of her eyes. Kari opened her mouth to speak, but a lump suddenly lodged in her throat, prohibited her from uttering a single word. It took her a few moments to gain her composure and with great effort, she managed to say,

"Wow Tess, I don't know what to say. I guess you want to go back outside and work on the flower garden. I am simply amazed at all you managed to do — all by yourself."

Trying very hard to keep her emotions in check, Kari felt that she was actually on the verge of losing that battle. She grabbed the handles of the wheelchair to use for support, when she suddenly felt her legs becoming weak and wobbly.

"Oh my Tess, you really surprised me today. I really didn't expect any of this. I thought that after being outside all day yesterday you might like to take a break. Now don't get me wrong, I am very happy to see that you are interested in our little project. Actually, I'm glad that we are going back out there today."

She started to push the wheelchair towards the door when she noticed that there was a plastic bag hanging on one of the handles. Peering inside, Kari found sunscreen, a couple of bottles of water and two apples. Smiling at Tess's forethought of packing the sunscreen along with the snack and drinks, she couldn't help but feel that a strong bond was forming between them.

CHAPTER 22

As Kari laid out the blanket near the flower garden, Tess remained in her wheelchair holding their cups of tea. Once things were situated, Kari took the two cups from Tess, which allowed the elderly woman the use of both her hands to get out of the chair on her own and make her way onto the blanket.

As Kari lowered herself to the ground, she wondered if today might be the day that Tess would finally break her silence and start to communicate verbally with her. Secretly she hoped that it was.

Taking the sunscreen out of the bag, she began to rub it on Tess's arms and neck and the large brim of her hat protected Tess's face from the sun. As she sipped her tea, she could not help but feel thrilled with the fact that in less than a week, she had managed to get this woman to trust her — not to mention, like her.

The two sat in silence for a while, enjoying the pleasant morning sounds. They heard a symphony of birds singing from the trees, commingled by the distant sounds of lawn mowers and a hint of far off traffic frolicked in the air too. However, what really caught her attention was, the scent of spring in the air and the sound of the gentle breeze that flowed through the trees that reminded her of the many summer vacations, so long ago, that she spent with her Aunt Gert.

Allowing her mind to wander, Kari soon was reminiscing about her childhood vacations. Her memories were clear visions, so clear in fact, that she could see her Aunt Gerties' hair blowing in the wind. The vision was so real; she felt that if she were to stretch out her hand, she could actually touch her.

Kari was so engrossed in her own thoughts, that she didn't even notice that Tess was no longer sitting on the blanket. It was not until she heard an odd, yet familiar sound, did she break from her thoughts. As she came back to reality, her heart skipped a beat when she became aware that Tess was gone. Gasping out of fear, she quickly bolted around to check her surroundings. Immediately, her panic subsided when she had seen that Tess had merely gotten up and headed over to the flower bed to resume their chore of pulling out the weeds.

"Tess, you gave me quite a scare. You could have let me know that you were going to get started you know, I was just daydreaming."

Saying nothing, Tess just continued to pull the weeds out and drop them, one by one, into the metal pail next to her. Grabbing her kneepad, Kari joined Tess in the dirt. The two of them working side by side, pulled the weeds and together they began transforming the old weed bed into a clean patch of dirt.

They worked well past lunch when, Kari decided that they had done enough for the day. She gathered up their tools and stored their belongings under a small tarp near the dirt patch. Tess helped by finding a few large rocks to place on the ends of the tarp so that if the wind kicked up, the tarp would stay put.

"Thank you Tess. Putting these rocks on here is a great idea." Kari glanced at her watch and was shocked at the time.

"Oh my goodness, I can't believe that we are late for lunch, I'm sorry about that Tess. I just can't believe I let time get away like that. I hope we don't get into too much trouble over this."

Tess just smiled and walked over to her wheelchair. Instead of sitting in it, she leaned over it to grab the bag that was still hanging on the handle. Slipping her hand into it, she retrieved two apples. She handed one to Kari and the other she kept for herself.

"Well, what do ya know. I forgot about the apples. I'm sorry that I didn't even think about grabbing those when I got us the bottles of water."

Tess began to rub her apple against her blouse, polishing it up. Before she put it to her mouth to take a bite, she noticed that Kari was doing the same thing. Tess took the moment in and began to smile — on the inside.

CHAPTER 23

For the first time in her working career, Kari felt that this day would never end. Ever since her dinner with Veeona, she couldn't get that horrible story out of her mind and she desperately wanted to get home to begin researching some of the stuff she learned.

After a full day of digging in the dirt, she managed to get Tess back into her room, cleaned up and even succeeded in getting her to eat all of her dinner. She was tired and ready for her shift to end. As she moved around the room, putting Tess's things in their proper place, she said,
"Tess, I think we had a very productive day today. I know that we certainly got a lot accomplished out there, that's for sure."

Picking up the food tray and wiping down the table, Kari then gathered Tess's dirty clothes, went to the closet and placed them in the hamper. While in there, she noticed, for the first time, a brown wooden box on the top shelf. With her curiosity peaked, she began to wonder if the contents of that box held the answers to Tess's clandestine life.
Not wanting Tess to catch her rummaging through her personal belongings, she quietly closed the closet door and continued with her one sided conversation. Hoping that, one of these days she just may say the right words that will cause Tess to break her silence and respond back to her.
"Man, I am beat tonight, you must be too. I'll bet that we both sleep like a log tonight. What do you think?" she asked.
Tess, who just emerged from the bathroom in her nightgown, grabbed her robe and put it on. Ignoring, or at least not responding to anything Kari was saying.
"Now I don't want you stay up too late, I know how you like to read your book or your paper at night. We still have a lot more work to do out there — if you feel up to it, that is, and I don't want you to be over tired tomorrow. Oh, I know tomorrow is Saturday and it's my day off, but I don't have anyone at home waiting on me; I never have and probably never will."

Tying her robe belt around her waist, Tess just walked past her, heading for her rocking chair. Grabbing her newspaper, she began flipping through it until she found the section she was looking for — the crossword puzzle.

"Well, alrighty then, I see you are all situated for now. I turned down the bed for you and placed a fresh bottle of water on your nightstand too. Is there anything else I can do for you before I leave for the night?"

Of course, there was no response; moreover, Tess didn't even look up at her, as she was getting ready to leave. This tugged at Kari's heart. Just when she thought that she was making some headway, breaking the walls down that Tess had surrounded herself with, she seemed to have built another one up. Feeling a little saddened by the lack of response, Kari left her to do her crossword puzzle and quietly slipped out of her room.

CHAPTER 24

For the first hour that she was home, Kari had been searching the internet trying to find something about the old prison. Not being very successful in her endeavors, she decided to head out to the public library.

Upon entering the building, she was greeted immediately by the scent of old books. Even though she had never been in this particular library before, the aroma was consistent with all the other libraries she had visited over the years. A scent so reminiscent that it reminded her of the many pleasurable evenings, of her past researches, that it seemed to be welcoming her home. She took a quick glance of the facility, assessing her surroundings. She knew she would be needing assistance before she could begin, so she headed directly to the information desk. Thankfully, the librarian was poised behind the counter, ready to assist her.

"Excuse me,' she said to the woman behind the counter 'can you help me?"

"Yes, what can I help you with?"

"Well, actually, I am wondering if you can direct me to your historical archives. I am doing some research on the Whispering Creek Assisted-Living building and was interested in any information that you may have."

"Alright, but first, do you have a library card?"

"No. Can I get one today?"

"Sure you can, just fill out this paper and then we can get started."

Kari filled out the document and handed it back to the librarian, who promptly keyed her information into her computer and within a few minutes, Kari was handed a plastic library card that looked like a credit card.

"Here you go Ms. Davies and welcome to Barrister Pines Library."

"Thank you. I'm sorry, what is your name?" she asked.

"Clara Watkins."

"Clara. I'm sorry, do you mind if I call you Clara?"

"No, not at all. Actually, I'd prefer it."

"And I'd prefer you call me Kari. No need to be so formal right?"

"No, not at all," she said. "So, you're interested in the history of what building?"

Kari wasted no time to explain what she was looking for. As soon as she brought up the fact that the State had converted Whispering Creek several times over the years, Clara became interested too.

"Really — Whispering Creek wasn't always an assisted-living home? I don't believe it."

"That's what I was told and that's why I am here — to research it."

"Alright then, follow me to the dungeon and you can get started. Now remember, we close at nine o'clock and tomorrow we open at eight A.M."

Kari followed the librarian to the back of the room where the stairway was located. As they descended the stairs to the basement, Kari was becoming a little nervous about being down there alone.

As they reached the bottom of the stairs, she was relieved to find at least a few people were sitting around the room, all at different tables. She presumed that, out of the six people studying down there, four of them had to be college students researching something for one of their classes. The other two, both men, she wasn't too sure about. One man, who looked to be in his seventies, was sitting in an armchair that was near a lamp. He was thumbing through a large book as if he was looking for something particular. The other man who looked to be more in his early fifties, was a handsome man. He was well dressed, muscular not fat, with dark wavy hair that was slightly graying at the temples and he had some nice looking stubble of unshaven facial hair. Just as she was about to peel her eyes from this man, she unintentionally ran into the back of the librarian who had come to a complete stop before her.

"Oh, I am so sorry Clara. I didn't see you stop," Kari whispered.

"I can see that, Kari. Don't worry, I'm not hurt. Come on, I'll show you where to find the microfilm. You do know how to work the microfilm machine, right?"

"It's been a long time, but I'm sure it will come back to me. No problem."

"Alright, follow me."

Clara led her to the back of the room where there were three machines against the wall. It became apparent to Kari that these machines haven't been used in a very long time, mainly because the three machines were protected with a plastic cover and they were full of dust.

"Wow, am I outdated or what?" Kari asked.

Smiling, Clara removed the dusty plastic cover from one of the machines and said,

"I don't think you are outdated Kari. It's just that these kids were born in the *'technological'* age and they prefer having information right at their fingertips." She glanced over her shoulder to look at the four college students then back at Kari then continued,

"Those kids over there have no idea how these machines work. Granted, they are probably researching things that we don't even have on microfilm, but, if a satellite ever falls out of the sky or the internet goes down, I'm sure I'll be teaching these youngsters a lesson on how research used to done."

They both started chuckling at the thought of such a catastrophe happening when Kari said,

"That would really be a dark day, wouldn't it?"

Clara set the machine up with the first of four rolls of microfilm that Kari and her located in the archives.

"OK, I've got you set up on the first one. Are you sure you're ok here?"

"Thank you Clara, I'll be fine."

"Alright, but if you need anything, come upstairs and get me. If the machine jams, just shut it down. The heat from the light bulb can melt the film and there is no way to replace it."

Kari nodded and whispered a thank you. Clara patted her on the shoulder, wished her good luck, and then left her to her own accord.

Kari glanced at her watch, noting that it was six o'clock. *'Oh geez, I only got three hours'* she thought. Quickly she got herself situated. She got her pen and pad of paper ready, then she began rolling through the film.

With every turn of the knob and the film advancing forward, the sound seemed deafening in such a quiet atmosphere. Several times she had glanced over her shoulder, to make sure that she wasn't disturbing the others, but in reality, the noise only bothered the four college kids.

One by one, they left the basement, in search for a quieter spot. The elderly man in the armchair remained and at some point, Kari thought he might have fallen sleep. She turned to see if the other man was still around and wondered if her noisy machine was disturbing him as well. As she glanced at the table where he was seated when she first entered the room, she was surprised to see that it was empty. Turning her head in the other direction, she found that the man was now sitting at a table that was directly behind her.

"Hello," he whispered to her.

Startled by this handsome man's sudden presence and not to mention, him greeting her, she suddenly became speechless.

"I'm sorry, did I frighten you?" he asked.

It took every muscle in her body to get her to open her mouth to speak. A mere millisecond of time passed, but to Kari, it felt like hours. Finally, she managed to utter a few intelligible words of her own.

"No, not really, I just wasn't expecting anyone to be sitting where you are. I'm sorry, is this machine disturbing you? I noticed that I single handedly managed to run some of the others off."

Smiling, the handsome man said,

"No, your machine is not disturbing me, but...."

"But what?" she asked.

"But, you seemed to have captured my attention and I no longer can concentrate on my work."

"Oh, I'm sorry. I'll be done here in a few minutes and then I'll shut it down."

"No, no. Please don't. I'm sorry, let me introduce myself." He got up from his seat, walked over to her with his hand extended and said, "My name is Tom."

Kari shook his hand and replied,

"Nice to meet you Tom, I'm Kari."

"Kari," he said with a smile, "pleasure to meet you too."

He continued to just stand there smiling at her, and as an awkward moment began to develop, Kari decided to ask,

"What type of work do you do, that requires the use of a library?"

"I was just going over some old land maps. My grandfather had been telling me for years about a parcel of land that belongs to him and before he dies, he wants to get things settled. He says that's part of my inheritance."

"Well, that sounds pretty important. Your grandfather is still alive then?"

"Yep, he's in his mid-nineties and I wouldn't be surprised if he made it to a hundred. He is one stubborn old coot," he chuckled. "But I love the old guy."

Tom peered over her shoulder, hoping to get a glimpse at what she was working on, but his attempt was in vain. Knowing that he sucked at being a super sleuth, he decided it would be best if he were up-front about his curiosity. Relying on his usual charm, he decided to just flat-out ask her,

"So, what are you working on? I haven't seen anyone use this type of machine in decades."

"Oh, nothing really, it's just a personal hobby of mine."

"Interesting, a hobby that requires outdated technology. Now my interests are peaked even more," he said.

Kari blushed like a schoolgirl. It had been a long time since a man had paid any attention to her, and she almost forgot how to behave.

"It's a long story, but what I'm looking for would require a fee if I were to search online. At least in the library, I don't have to pay for anything, unless of course I want some pages printed. Free is always a good price to pay, don't you agree?" she asked.

"Absolutely, free is always a great price!"

He hemmed and hawed for a moment and then asked,

"You know, I haven't seen you around here before, are you new to the area?"

"Uh, yes. Actually, I just moved into the vicinity a few weeks ago."

"Oh? How nice, well let me welcome you to our neck of the woods then."

Smiling at his charm, Kari noticed for the first time that he had incredibly dark brown eyes, adorned with long black lashes. Captured within the darkness of his eyes were specks of gold that when a glint of light hit them, they sparkled. She was shocked and surprised that she felt a flutter in her stomach; it had been such a long time since the sight of a man had stirred any excitement within her.

"Well, thank you Tom. I'll consider you to be the town ambassador and its official spokesman. On behalf of myself, I thank you for the official welcome."

They both started quietly laughing when they heard someone clearing their throat. The older man in the armchair was letting them know that they were getting too loud and that they were disturbing him. Tom waved a hand at him, signaling that they will be quieter and quickly turned his attention back to Kari.

"I figured that the old guy would have just gotten up and left," he said.

"You know, he had been in the same position so long; I thought that he had fallen asleep."

Once again, they both started laughing, but this time they quieted down much quicker.

"I'm sorry Kari, I didn't mean to disturb you and keep you from your... hobby. I probably should get back to my own work too."

He walked back to the table behind her and started to gather up his papers when he said,

"Kari, would you have a coffee with me after you are done here?"

A little stunned about a perfect stranger asking her out, she wasn't sure how to respond. Her insides were screaming 'Yes, yes, yes' but, her head was trying to figure out a way to politely decline his offer.

"Well, I planned on being here until the library closed. I kind of have a tight time schedule."

Shuffling his papers from one hand to the other, trying to make it look like he was picking his things up then, he tried one more time to get her to accept his invitation.

"You didn't say no so, that means I still have a chance here." He shot her a quick smile then said,

"I don't have a problem working until nine, I might actually get something accomplished by that time myself," he laughed.

"Mmmm.... all right, I guess I could get a cup of coffee afterwards, but I can't stay out late. I have a really busy day tomorrow and I have to be up early."

Grinning from ear to ear, he said,

"Great, you just continue on with your research and I'll go sit across the room and get my stuff done, how's that?"

The butterflies in her stomach came back and soon, she too had a big smile on her face.

"OK, that sounds like a great plan. Then I guess I'll talk with you later."

"That sounds like a superb plan, now will the two of you kindly shut up!"

Both Tom and Kari looked across the room at the old man in the armchair. He gave them both a look of disgust and promptly turned his attention back to the book that he had been reading. Kari turned to Tom, as he did the same and once their eyes met, they both erupted in uncontrollable chuckling. Tom, who was still laughing, grabbed his papers and moved away from the table. Once he got control of himself, he turned to the old man and said,

"I'm sorry, sir. We won't interrupt you again. See I'm moving all the way over here and this lovely woman will stay where she is. We will both stay very quiet for the rest of the evening. I promise."

"Then shut up already," the old man barked.

"It's shut. There will be no more talking. Um, I'm done now, for real."

"Good!" he said quite angrily. "Maybe now there will be some peace and quiet around here," he finished, as he once again turned his attention back to his book.

CHAPTER 25

Flipping papers back and forth, Tom wasn't getting anything accomplished. Kari consumed his every thought and he found it difficult to concentrate on the pages before him. He found that he was very attracted to her, which to him was quite an amazing feat. He was not the type of man to have feelings like that, especially towards a perfect stranger.

Tom, a widower in his late forties, hadn't looked at or had been interested in another woman in over twenty-five years. After the death of his wife, he felt that he could never love another woman again, not as he had loved Donna. Her death had taken a huge toll on him. In reality, the day she died was the day he quit living.

For the past five years, he was doing nothing more than just existing. The sun would rise in the morning and he would get up for work. The sun would set in the evening and he would choke down some food that slightly resembled a meal. When dinner was done, he'd go off to bed, waiting for the next sunrise to come, just to do it all over again.

As his mind seesawed back and forth, from Donna to Kari then back again, he felt deep within his heart, for the first time, that Donna would be OK with him moving on. All kinds of new feelings were mulling around inside of him, feelings that he was not even sure he should be having.

He caught himself glancing up and seeing her sitting across the room and every time he looked at her, he started to get excited. He hadn't had an ache in his groin for a long time, and it took him by great surprise. In fact, it had been so long, he was afraid he might not be able to control his bodily functions. Having an erection was one thing, but a premature ejaculation in his pants was something altogether different. Before an accident could happen, Tom got up to go to the restroom. He seriously hoped that a little cold water might help settle things back down. *'At least the little guy still works,'* he thought, as he walked to the bathroom.

While washing his hands in cold water, he glanced into the mirror and noticed he was smiling. It had been a long time for that to happen too. Seeing a smile on his face seemed a little foreign to him anymore, but he did like how his face looked when he wore one.

A sense of relief came over him, when he felt his erection finally subsiding; now all he had to do was to make sure that it didn't happen again, especially while they were out having a coffee.

Checking his watch for the time, he was pleased to see that closing time was only fifteen minutes away. He started to gather up his papers and pack them into his leather briefcase. Keeping them safe until the next time he came to the library. After clearing up his table, he noticed the old man across the room had risen from his chair. He returned his book to its proper shelf and headed towards the stairwell to leave. Tom watched his every move wondering if the old man would leave quietly, but as the old man reached the stairway, he turned in their direction and said,

"I'm leaving now. You two knuckleheads can now make as much noise as you feel is necessary."

Slowly he turned back and climbed the stairs to the main level, within moments he was gone.

Kari, who had been so engrossed in what she was doing, turned from her microfilm machine and asked,

"What was that all about?"

"Who knows, the old goat has anger issues."

He started heading towards Kari when he asked,

"Are you about ready to get out of here? The library will be closing in three minutes."

"Oh crap, I have to put all this away. I need more than three minutes."

"Don't you worry about that, Clara will put them away."

"Do you think that she might keep them out for me? I think I may come back tomorrow or on Sunday."

"I don't know, come on, let's go ask her."

Hesitating for a brief moment, Kari quickly grabbed her stuff and shoved it all into her canvas bag. After double-checking her area, to make sure that she wasn't leaving anything personal behind, she and Tom headed for the stairs.

Emerging from the stairwell, Tom and Kari headed straight for the main library desk where they found Clara tidying up her area for the evening. Out of the corner of her eye, Clara caught a glimpse of someone approaching and immediately turned her attention to the on-comers. Recognizing who they were, she smiled and said,

"Have a good evening Tom, were you able to make any headway in your search tonight?"

"I may have gotten a step closer, but to actually say I've accomplished something...No. You will not be rid of me yet Clara, I will be back."

He flashed his most charming smile at her and that made her blush. Seeing Kari standing just off to the side of him, she asked,

"Oh Kari, I'm sorry, I didn't see you there. How did everything go, did you find all you were looking for?"

"No, not really Clara, but I do have a request."

"Sure honey, what do you need?"

"Well, I left all the rolls of film out on the table where I was working and I was wondering if you can either save them or leave them their until tomorrow. I will have to come back and look through some more film. Is that something you can do?"

"Sure I can. Actually, I will gather them up and keep them here on my desk, so that when you come back in, all you have to do is come and see me. See, there is no problem honey, I'll take care of it."

Relieved, Kari thanked her and told her that she would be seeing her in the morning.

Wishing them both a pleasant evening, Clara watched as they headed towards the exit. Glancing over his should, Tom shot Clara a wink, as Kari walked through the door that he was holding open for her.

CHAPTER 26

The coffee shop was less than a block away from the library and Tom managed to talk Kari into walking the short distance with him. As they strolled along, he made small talk, telling her little insignificant details about the town. Recounting some stories he remembered hearing from his grandfather.

When he was younger, he really didn't care about the history of the town, but now, he wished he had paid better attention to his grandfather's stories.

They arrived at the coffee shop and took a booth next to the window, each sitting on opposite sides. The waitress, who was probably no more than eighteen years old, was standing at their table ready to take their order.

"What can I get you folks?" she asked.

Tom took the liberty to order for the both of them,

"We'll just have two coffees"

"Would you like cream?"

"Yes please," he said.

She scurried off to retrieve two cups and a pot of fresh brewed coffee. She returned within minutes with their order and as quickly as she came, she was gone.

"Wow, that was quick" Kari remarked.

"Yeah, that's what I like about this place, their coffee and their quick service."

As he added the cream and sugar in his cup, thoughts were racing through his mind, trying to find the best way to start a pleasant conversation between them. He couldn't make up his mind as to what would be best to start with.

Kari too had been thinking about what they were going to talk about, but she noticed that the man sitting across from her was not the same confident man that he had been when he approached her in the basement of the library. He seemed a little uncomfortable and now unsure what to do next. Smiling inside, she decided not to let him suffer any longer, so she instigated the conversation herself.

"So, have you lived here all your life?"

A sense of relief swept over him, as he heard her voice. Looking from his cup to her eyes, he replied,

"For the most part, I have. I left for a few years to go to college but, like everyone else in this town, I came back. We all come back — one way or another."

"I see. So what is it that you do for a living? It can't be just hanging around a library's basement; waiting for single women to show up so that you can ask them out for coffee, is it?"

"So are you?" he charmingly asked.

"Am I what?"

"Single. I didn't notice a ring on your finger back at the library, but I probably should have asked you at that time — sorry."

"No need to be sorry Tom," she said. "And to ease your curious mind, yes, I am single."

His smile turned inquiringly. He wondered how could such an adorable creature as this, possibly still be single. Fearing that he might be delving into waters he shouldn't be, he chose a softer, yet simpler route in his quest in getting to know her.

"So, what kind of work do you do?"

"I'm a caregiver at an assisted-living home."

"Really? So you work over at Whispering Creek?"

"How did you know that?"

"Um, do you think it may be because it's the only one in the area? I don't know, I'm just saying..." he chuckled.

A little embarrassed, Kari's cheeks started to heat up and her color went from a normal flesh tone to one with a hint of blush. She could feel the heat of her embarrassment rise from her neck all the way up to her forehead.

"Well, I guess the old saying is correct."

"What saying is that?" he questioned.

"You learn something new every day. Heard of that one?" she smiled at him.

"As a matter of fact, yes I have. So, how long have you been an aide and what made you decide to get into that type of work?"

"Professionally, a little more than fifteen years now, but I guess you could say forever. I have been taking care of the elderly all my life. I think I just always liked being around older people. They have so many wonderful stories about the past and for the most part, their lives were so interesting. To see their eyes light up when they reminisce about their younger days, it's priceless. Sometimes, I wish I had a time machine, so that I could travel back in time and witness firsthand what they had experienced."

He noticed how excited she became as she talked about the people under her care. He never really thought much of the elderly, but the more he listened to her, the more interested he became.

"When I was a little girl, I remember my mother bringing me to my Aunt Gert's lake house. We used to spend the summers out there and I absolutely loved it. I remember that from the minute mom and I showed up, my job was to go and collect the rocks for the fire pit. I'd jump out of the car, run to give Aunt Gert a hug and off to the lake shore I'd go. I'd have the all rocks gathered and set in place in about an hour or so, then I would head back to the house for dinner. Like clockwork, the second we were done with dinner, I would start begging my mom and aunt to hurry and start the fire.

Eventually, I figured out that Aunt Gert used to throw all the rocks from the previous year's pit, into a couple of choice spots so it would be easier for me to gather. I never let on that I knew her secret, I just let her throw them out there, year after year."

"I bet that was fun. I remember my grandfather telling me that we used to camp out in the summers when I was small. Unfortunately, I can't remember any of it. He did tell me we used to go every year until I was at least five."

"Oh? Why did he stop?"

"Not sure really, I'll have to ask him when I get home. After hearing your story, I think maybe I should at least try and find out — before it's too late."

"Well, if you have the opportunity to find out, you should. I'm sure your grandfather has some remarkable stories that you ought to hear, before he takes them with him when he passes on. You know, you will never get a chance like this again, once he's gone that is."

"I know. You're right, I should ask him. I should know things about my family and my past."

He looked into her eyes and for the second time in a single day, he found that he was getting aroused. It had been so many years since the mere sight of a woman had excited him, he knew he liked her right away, but he had no idea that he would like her so much that he didn't want the evening to end.

"So you never told me, why were you so eager to get the fire going?"

Before she answered him, a smile crept across her face, as the memories of the lake house came flooding back to her.

"Because, when the fire was fully ablaze, all the other grownups would come. I used to think that we were sending out smoke signals, you know. When the neighbors would see the fire, or the smoke rising in the sky, it was like their cue to show up. The smoke signal was our way of letting them know that the coast was clear and it was safe for them to come on over. Sometimes, there would be as many as ten people out there, but usually, there were only four or five. We would all be sitting around the fire and once everyone had a drink, the grownups with their beer, and I with a soda, story time would begin. I could listen to them tell stories for hours. They could have told me the same story a dozen times, and I'd listen to it as if it was the first time. Sometimes, the re-run stories were even better," she laughed.

Tom had no idea how beautiful she really was, until that very moment that she broke into laughter. He loved how the light danced in her eyes, like the brightest of stars twinkling in the night's dark sky. He enjoyed seeing her face light up when she spoke of the past as well. Not only did he relish in what she had to say, he truly enjoyed hearing her voice too. She spoke in a soft and gentle tone and the sounds coming out of her mouth was like, music to his ears.

After listening to her talk about the past, it made him to think of his own youth. He never took story time to heart, not like her. He had no interest in the past. In fact, he vaguely remembered his own childhood with his parents and grandfather. Not that it was a bad time, but it just wasn't his personality to remember such things. He told Kari that he camped out with his grandfather, not because it was a memory, but because his grandfather had told him that they had.

"So did you learn anything interesting from all those stories?" he asked.

"I know that some of the stories were cut short once in a while. I think that they didn't want me to hear them and sometimes I would see that my mother would get upset. By the time I was old enough, we had already stopped going to the lake house and a year before I graduated from college; Aunt Gert died."

"I'm sorry," he said, as he slipped his hand across the table and placed in on top of hers. Kari didn't pull her hand away, even though the butterflies began dancing the cha-cha in the pit of her stomach.

"Thank you Tom but, that was a long time ago. So many things have happened since then and besides, I still get my fill of stories from the seniors in the home. Their stories are as important to me as, a pusher is to a junkie. Every one of those senior citizens has a never-ending chasm full of real life stories. They need to tell their stories, and I believe that somebody needs to hear and be witness to them as well. Letting these people die, taking their stories to their grave, without anyone ever knowing about them, is almost criminal in my book."

"Wow, I never really thought of it that way. So, your research, it has to do with one of the seniors in the home?"

Kari hesitated, uncertain if she should divulge any information to him. After all, he is a perfect stranger that she just met a few hours ago.

"Well…sort of," she said.

"Oh come on Kari, you have successfully tapped into an area of my curiosity that my own grandfather could never reach, you start telling me a fascinating story and then quit before the end. That's not right," he exclaimed.

Surprised at his outburst, Kari hadn't expected him to really be interested in what she was saying, but by the way he looked and sounded, she couldn't believe that he really was.

She had a moment of clarity and in that moment, she had a revelation. As he stared at her, her mind went into overdrive, as she thought; *OMG, I just found someone that actually is interested in something that interests me too.* Her heart began to flutter and her mouth went dry. She wanted to speak, but her tongue was stuck to the roof of her mouth. She grabbed her cup of coffee and carefully brought it to her lips. She hoped that the wetness of the coffee would unseal her seemingly glued lips. Relief washed over her as she took the first sip. Her tongue was now free to move about inside her mouth. Taking another large sip for good measure, she then said,

"I really didn't tell you anything, Tom. I was just reminiscing about my childhood and how I got interested in hearing about other people's life stories."

"What are you talking about Kari? You were telling me your life's story right now. One doesn't need to be old, or better yet, ancient, to have a life story. You have one, I have one. Hell, even that young server of ours has one — granted it wouldn't be as interesting as some of the really old people that you talk to, but still, she has one."

Pondering on what he just said, Kari really had not thought of it that way. What she marveled at was just how passionate and sincere he remained.

"That's true. I guess I never thought of it that way, sorry."

Smiling at her, as he once again slid his hand across the table to place it on top hers, he said,

"Apology accepted. So, I know you plan on going back to the library tomorrow, would you mind if I joined you?"

Kari didn't expect to hear that question. Even though she was elated that this handsome man sitting across from her, wanted to see her again, she wasn't sure what to do. She hadn't been in the dating world for ages and here she was, a middle-aged woman acting like a young schoolgirl. The butterflies in her gut were banging into her stomach wall so hard that her heart began to race, as if she were a track runner on steroids.

"Well," she managed to say, "the library is a public place — and I don't think I can actually keep you out of a public place — right?"

"Although that may be true Kari, what I am asking is — can I see you again?"

She answered before she could talk herself out of it.

"Yes, I'd like that very much. I would like to see you again too. I'll be at the library around eleven."

That was when it dawned on her to look at the wall clock.

Seeing that it was almost midnight, she exclaimed,

"Oh my, look at the time. I have to get back Tom, it's really late."

"Wow, did we really just sit here and talk for three hours? It feels like we just got here, doesn't it?"

She hated to admit it, but yes. She too could have stayed longer, if only she didn't have to go to work in the morning.

They walked back to the parking lot of the library and Tom escorted her to her car. He stood outside her car door and waited for her to start the engine, then he watched her as she pulled away. He stood in the parking lot as she maneuvered her car out of the lot and out onto the road, before he headed for his own car.

As he sat behind the wheel in complete silence, he replayed the evening in mind. He couldn't get the vision of her face out of his head and he didn't want to either. He found her to be an amazing woman and an extremely beautiful one too. The more he thought of her, the more aroused he became. Though this time, he wasn't going to fight it. He let his body do what it wanted to do. After all, it was a natural reaction and besides, he hadn't had a hard on for a very long time and it was good to know that nothing was broken and that he wasn't dead, at least from the waist down that is.

"What could be better?" he asked himself aloud, "Oh, I know what could be better...but that, will have to wait." Smiling, he put his car in gear and drove home.

CHAPTER 27

After tossing and turning all night long, Kari managed to get up and out the door by six in the morning. She headed straight to work, so she could spend some time with Tess. As she walked down the hallway, Melva called out,

"What are you doing here Kari? Isn't this your day off?"

"Yes, but I promised Tess that I would be back today. I'm just visiting for a few hours and then I'll be gone."

"Alright, but I really think you ought to take advantage of your time off. Sometimes, you may not get the chance, especially when you may need it."

"Thanks Melva, I will definitely make a note of that — I promise."

Knocking lightly on Tess's door before entering the room, Kari found Tess was already up and sitting in her rocker by the window. Next to the rocker was a folding chair, it had been set there as an invitation for someone to sit down and join her by the window. Not waiting for a verbal invitation that she knew would never come, Kari went over and sat down in the empty chair.

"Good morning Tess, I brought us a cup of tea."

Tess put her crossword puzzle down and took one of the cups from Kari. They sat for a few minutes in silence, when all of a sudden; Kari felt the need to share her incredible evening with her.

"You won't believe what happened to me last night, Tess. I still can't believe it myself. Hell, I don't think I even slept a wink last night."

Her face was nothing but smiles and as Tess looked at her, she couldn't help but smile too.

"I met the most gorgeous man last night. He was a complete gentleman, through and through. He asked me to join him for a cup of coffee and I almost told him no. I am so glad that I didn't. His name is Tom... Oh my,' she looked dumbfounded, 'I never got his last name. I am such an idiot, Tess. I cannot believe I never asked him for his last name."

She began to laugh and then it turned into a giggle, as if she were a teenager again. Her excitement seemed to have been contagious because, Tess couldn't wait to hear more.

"Anyway, after I left here, I went to the library. I was snooping around in the old records department and this handsome fellow kept switching tables until he was right next to mine. He started making small talk at first and before I knew it, he asked me if I'd like to have a coffee with him. We walked to the coffee shop that was only two, maybe three buildings away and before I knew it, three hours had slipped by. But, do you want to hear the best part? He asked to see me again, today! Can you believe it?

I never would have thought that at my age I would ever attract any man. Actually, after Alan , I didn't think that I would ever be interested in another man again. Oh, but Tess, this man, he is truly something. He's extremely good looking, around my age and he seemed interested in some of the same things that I'm interested in. That's like hitting the Trifecta at the horse races! I've never hit a trifecta or even picked a winning horse in my life.

Oh my, I just can't believe it. I've had butterflies in my belly since last night. I blushed just like a schoolgirl and it took all of my will power not to jump his bones when he walked me back to my car last night."

Tess's eyes lit up and as well as her smile, but Kari was floating so high on cloud nine as she was telling her story that she didn't even notice.

"Tess, I know I told you yesterday that we would work on the flower garden today, but would you mind terribly if we didn't? There are two reasons; one, I don't want you to get over exerted and two, I have a date in a couple of hours."

Kari was so excited she could hardly contain herself and that was when Tess placed her cup of tea down on the little table next to her rocker. Taking Kari's hands into her own, she gave them a gently squeeze and then pointed to the door, motioning Kari to go away.

"What's the matter Tess? Is something wrong?"

Tess shook her head no, but continued to wave her out.

"Are you telling me that it's OK for me to skip our date today so I can go meet this new fabulous man?"

The only way Tess could make Kari understand what she was trying to say was to get out of her chair, grab her by the hand, and pull her towards the door. Once there, Tess opened it and pushed her into the hallway. As she stood on the other side of the door, Kari was speechless. Smiling, Tess waved good-bye and quietly closed the door in her face.

Wasting no time, Kari turned on her heals and headed for the exit. She had just enough time to get home, change into something a little more comfortable before heading off to the library.

CHAPTER 28

Clara busied herself with putting the returned books back onto the shelves, carefully checking each one to make sure there was no damage done to them. She hated it when people would bring the books back in horrible shape

As she picked up each book, she gently slid her hand over the top and the bottom, feeling for gouges or tears in the covers. Then she would fan through the pages to make sure there were no ripped or torn pages. And God forbid, the occasional pen or pencil marks underlining specific sentences or paragraphs that someone noted. For the life of her, she could never figure out how people could be so selfish and rude about destroying public property. Every time she would find one of the books destroyed by the carelessness of these so-called, upstanding citizens, she just wanted to grab them by the neck and choke them.

Books have always been a very important part of her life. She treasured every one that had passed through her hands, and had always been very adamant that others treat them with regard as well. To her, reading a book was like peeking through a window into another time or place, or better yet, into someone else's life. Depending on what type of book she was reading, the stories offered her an escape from her own mundane everyday life.

Fortunately, Clara hadn't found any damaged books — yet. Nevertheless, she knew that as the day progressed, she would eventually run across one or two that someone had defaced.

As she carefully placed each book back onto its proper shelf, a recognizable eerie squeaking sound broke the silence in the room. Instinctively, Clara recognized the sound at once. Someone has opened the front door and entered the library. With her trained ear, she listened to the footsteps of the visitor, as they crossed the main floor. Their heels making a clacking sound against the tiled floor had abruptly come to a stop.

Clara had no fear, she had worked in the library long enough to recognize the many different sounds that were associated with the library and the old building itself. She instinctively knew that the visitor was now waiting for her at the main desk, obviously in need of her assistance.

Setting the books down on the cart, she headed to the front desk to see whom it was that needed her help. As she emerged into view, she had seen that it was Kari. Her face lit up instantly as she quickened her pace, so that she wouldn't keep her waiting any longer.

"Hi Kari, glad you came back today," she said.

"Hi Clara, yeah, I hoped to try and get some more research done today."

She was looking around the library, hoping that Tom would be there, but her heart had sunk a little when there was no sight of him.

"Did you happen to notice if Tom had come in yet?"

"Why no I haven't. Was he planning on coming in today?"

Kari began to explain how they met downstairs last night, then told her how he asked her out for coffee when they left the library. She told her how they both chatted long into the night and that he mentioned that he was planning on stopping in, in the morning.

Clara wasn't surprised to hear the excitement in Kari's voice in regards to Tom. After all, he was the town's most valuable catch and yet he was so elusive. She herself, along with most of the women in the town, had tried to win his affections. He was always a gentleman, but was never interested in any of the women that crossed his path. There were whispers circulating around town that he may possibly be gay, but Clara knew the truth. His wife was everything to him. When she died, the fire in him died with her. It was nice to know that someone new was trying to become part of his life. Hoping that someone could finally break down the protective wall that he built around himself. Secretly she wished Kari good luck and hoped she could do what no other woman before her could do, snare the most sought after man in town.

"Do you have the rolls of film handy Clara?" Kari asked. "I think I ought to get started, if you don't mind."

"Sure thing, I have them all right here. I don't think anybody has been down there yet. I'll come with you to make sure the lights are on."

The two women headed for the stairs, with Clara in the lead. As they got the bottom of the stairwell, Clara flicked all the light switches into the *ON* position and within moments, the basement was full of light.

"There you go, that's much better, isn't it?" Clara remarked.

"Yes, thank you."

"I don't get too many chances to come down here." Clara says, "It is a little tough when the council will only allow one librarian to work at a time. I just don't get how they expect us to watch the front door and help the people, all at the same time. Let alone; help people like you, someone that has to work in the basement. I'm sure glad that you didn't run into any trouble with the machine last night, because that would have been a challenge to fix your machine and tend to the front desk. Hopefully, we will have a repeat of last night's good fortune."

"I sure hope so." Kari smiled, as a tiny little butterfly moved within her gut. A repeat of last night was exactly what she was looking forward to.

As Kari busied herself scrolling through the microfilm, she found that she was not as focused as she hoped to be. She found herself constantly turning in her seat, checking to see if Tom had shown up yet, but nothing other than disappointment greeted her.

She decided to force herself to forge ahead and immerse herself fully into her research, after all, that was the initial reason to be in the library in the first place. Now, with all her attention totally focused on her real cause, she stumbled across an old article about the jail – which read;

Warden Found Dead, Murder or Justice?

Warden, D. Percy Booker, found late last night. Booker was sitting behind the wheel of his black, '41 Studebaker that was parked on the side of the road, near the gates of the town's cemetery. Police are investigating the scene.

Booker had been the warden at the Elizabeth Lake Prison since it began its operations back in 1936. Last week a shake down at the prison had brought some unsavory light on the institution and onto some of the police officials working there. Booker was abruptly fired and brought up on countless charges of rape, false imprisonment, misuse of power from a person of authority and embezzlement at the state level, just to name a few.

A confidential source has disclosed that, Dewey Percy Booker, former warden of the prison, had been shot and killed. He suffered a single gunshot to the heart, and two shots to his head. In addition, the perpetrator had stabbed him in the groin, leaving the victim pinned to the seat. A single pink carnation, found lying in the victim's lap, may possibly be a calling card or a memento, investigators believe. At this time, police are under pressure, as no witnesses to the brutal crime are in sight.

Confirmation of these allegations cannot be confirmed as of yet, the police will not comment, nor will they release any details of this brutal crime.

Not sure if this article was going to be of any use, Kari hit the print key to take a copy of the old newspaper clipping.

As the printer spewed out the reproduction of an article that nobody has read in decades, Kari continued advancing the microfilm forward to see what else she could find. As she jotted down a couple of notes on her notepad, she heard,

"So how is our local sleuth doing today?"

Without having to turn to see who was there, Kari smiled, inside and out, as she replied,

"Sleuthing is hard work in case you didn't know."

She turned around to see that not only did Tom look even better in the daylight; he showed up with two cups of coffee as well.

"Well, well, what do we have here?" she asked.

"I come bearing gifts," he handed her one of the coffees and then produced a small bag, which contained two blueberry muffins, from under his arm.

"I figured that I would show up here a little later, you know, to give you some actual time to get your work done. I hope you like blueberries," he said, as he handed her one.

"Why thank you, I love blueberries."

"Great! That's good to know. So, were you able to find any information from your dinosaur machine?"

"Yes, I did. It has been very helpful in my quest."

"Oh, now it's a quest that you are on, huh? Anything you might like to share?"

"Not yet, but I do have a question for you though. I found an old article and as I read it over, I noticed that the reporter didn't list his name on the story. I find that a bit odd, don't you?"

"Yes, that is odd. Do you know what newspaper the article came from?"

She went to the printer to retrieve her paper, and upon her return, she handed it to Tom.

"Are you sure you want me to read this? I mean, once I see it, I may find out what it is you are looking into, you know."

"I'm aware of that, but I figured that it wouldn't hurt to maybe have an assistant help me out once in a while either," she said, as she turned on her charm.

Tom took the sheet of paper from her and began to read it. When he finished, he scanned it over, from top to bottom, hoping that there might be a clue as to what newspaper ran the article.

"Well?" she asked.

After several long moments of silence, as he stared at the paper, he said,

"Well Ms. Kari, we seem to have a real mystery on our hands."

"Now that is what I call true detective work Mr. Tom!" They both began to chuckle.

"OK, all kidding aside, where on the roll of film did you find this article? Do you think that you can find it again?"

"I think so, come on, let's look together."

Pulling a second chair over to the table where she had been working, Tom took a seat next to her. As she began scrolling through the film, and with Tom sitting so close to her, she suddenly found that she was no longer in a big hurry to find the article after all.

Tom's eyes were on the screen, but his mind was on the woman next to him. As he leaned in to see the screen a little better, he got a whiff of her perfume. The scent of her pleased him very much. He had no idea that he would have become so attracted to someone in such a short period of time, but he sure was glad that he took the chance last night at meeting her. Not to mention how glad he was that she accepted his offer to have coffee with him too. It had been a long time since he had asked a woman out; he was in fear of getting back into the dating scene. Nevertheless, since meeting Kari, he never gave his fear another thought. The only thought consuming him now was, when he would be able to see her again.

As he refocused his attention back to the microfilm machine, his eyes ran across a headline in the print. Without hesitation, he reached out for the controller knob and placed his hand on top of hers. As soon as they touched, he felt his heart skip a beat. When his fingers slipped through hers in order to rewind the film, his heart began to race.

Her skin was soft to the touch, but what he really made him happy was — she didn't pull away. Slowly, he rolled the knob backwards, passing only one frame at a time, because touching her, woke something deep within him that even he forgot existed — excitement.

Eventually, he came across the article that Kari had printed off. "Aha!" he said. "Here it is."

Reluctantly, he lifted his hand from hers and as he smiled at her, he thought for a brief moment that he saw deep within her eyes that they had made a connection. A spark, an ever so small glint of energy, exploded inside him and he couldn't help but smile. A feeling such as this had not happened to him in a very, very long time.

"OK, now that we found it again detective, what are we going to do with it?"

Composing himself and trying to remain the suave character he so effortlessly portrays, he said,

"Well my dear, here is where good sleuthing comes in handy. First, you look at the neighboring articles and see if you can find the name of the newspaper listed on them. If you can, then there is a good chance that your article came from the same paper. Actually, there should be an index somewhere on here, showing a listing for the, who, what, and where of things that pertain to this article to."

"Sounds like you have done this before," she says.

Turning slightly towards her, he confidently looked her in the eye when he sheepishly replied,

"Busted! Guilty as charged!" His shoulders dropped as he tilted his head down and lightheartedly continued, "I confess — I had used this old dinosaur a time or two. But, in my defense, it was a long, long time ago."

"Mmmm Hmmm, what, like last week?" she teasingly asked.

"No, more like a month ago, honest."

Shaking her head, Kari rolled her eyes while she laughed at him. Without realizing what she was doing, she had tilted her head and softly rested it upon his shoulder. Not wanting the moment to end, but knowing that it would, Tom took the opportunity to whisper to her,

"Have dinner with me tonight."

CHAPTER 29

After a fun filled afternoon, Kari hurried on home to change her clothes. She surprised herself by accepting Tom's invitation to have dinner with him later that evening, and even though they had spent almost the whole morning and most of the afternoon together, the mere thought of having dinner with him, excited her even more.

Rummaging through her closet, trying to find the perfect outfit for her date, Kari was flabbergasted that this task was much more difficult than she expected. After throwing most of her outfits onto her bed in disgust, she realized that she hadn't been on a date in a very long time, and by the looks of her wardrobe, it showed.
Deciding on a cute little floral skirt and a white sheer blouse to match, she quickly started getting herself ready for her date. Once fully dressed, she peered into the full-length mirror to get a good look at herself. She concluded that the outfit that she had thrown together looked perfect, except for one minor detail; her sheer blouse was just a bit too sheer. Not quite the message she wanted to send out, especially on a first date. *Although, that wouldn't be a bad idea*, she mused. Nevertheless, without a second thought, she headed straight to her lingerie drawer to find her silky white camisole.

She couldn't remember the last time that she had gotten all dressed up for a special occasion. It had been years since she had gone out. The last man that she had dinner with was Derek, and that had been so long ago, it was difficult to remember even him.

Fumbling through her lingerie drawer, she finally came across her camisole. After a moment of hesitation — contemplating whether to put it on or not, she quickly slipped it on, underneath her top. She had no intention of sending the wrong message to her date.

Now that she was fully dressed — again, she returned to the mirror to see if she looked as good as she felt. Pleased with the view, she ran her fingers through her hair, put on a light colored lip-gloss and headed out of her room.

Just as she finished fluffing the pillows along the couch, there was a knock at the front door. Within seconds, the butterflies in her gut started to kamikaze into the wall of her stomach. She had to take a quick deep breath to try to calm her excitement down, but instead, she found herself breaking into a run towards the front door.

"Don't be an idiot Kari, get a hold of yourself," she said, scolding herself quietly.

As she placed her hand onto the doorknob, she took another breath for good measure. This time she held it until she counted to three, then she opened the front door.

"Hi Tom, come on in," she said, as naturally as she could muster, considering the excitement swirling around inside her.

Upon entering her home, Tom immediately felt welcomed by the surroundings of her place.

"Nice cozy little home you have here."

"Thank you. It's a little small but, I don't need a lot of room; it's just me you know."

There was a moment of awkward silence when Tom looked at her and again he was stunned at how beautiful she really was.

"You look absolutely beautiful," he told her. His smile brightened up the room as he brought his hand from behind his back to present her with a bouquet of fresh cut flowers. Blushing with surprise, Kari cried out,

"Oh my, they are absolutely beautiful, thank you."

She took the flowers from his hand and before she could tilt the bouquet toward her to sniff their fragrance, the aroma of the fresh flowers had already filled the air. Her eyes drifted back over to Tom when she too, noticed how handsome he looked. Her insides started to twist and her heart started to pound in her chest. She couldn't remember ever feeling like this, not even when she dated Derek.

"You look very handsome tonight too," she said. "Nice suit."

"What, this old thing? Hell, this is so old, they probably don't even make this type of suit anymore," he chuckled.

"That is not an old suit. And even if it were, it certainly looks very nice on you," she winked.

"Well thank you, but please, let's not turn this into a fashion show argument either," he said with a smile. "Are you ready to go?"

"I sure am, just let me put these beautiful flowers into a vase, and then we can leave."

CHAPTER 30

After parking the car and cutting the engine, he turned to Kari and asked,

"I hope you like Italian, I probably should have asked you before, but..."

"Tom, stop worrying, I love Italian food. Everything will be fine," she smiled.

He got out of the car and quickly went over to open her door. Once she was out, she slipped her hand into the crook of his arm so they could walk in together. Tom didn't skip a beat; he just stood a little taller and was filled with pure gratification. Just knowing that such a beautiful creature as Kari was hanging on his arm; filled him with utter delight. It was a joy he had not had the pleasure of feeling, since Donna died.

Upon entering the restaurant, the hostess seated them right away. She picked a cozy little table for two, which was set in the far back corner of the restaurant. As they settled in their seats and began looking over the menu, the waiter arrived, to take their drink order.

"Would you please bring us your finest bottle of wine," he asked.

"Most certainly, sir." the waiter said.

As he disappeared into the back room to retrieve the wine and some glasses, Tom struggled for something to say. Kari, sensing her date, the man who had been so self-assured since the first time that they had met, looked a bit nervous. Feeling a bit uncomfortable herself, but feeling worse for him, decided to help him out by saying,

"This looks like a nice place. Do you eat here often?"

"I've been here a time or two," he managed to choke out.

"I see, so, why don't you tell me a little bit about yourself."

"What is it that you want to know?" He smiled brightly, now that his confidence was returning.

"Well for starters, you're not married are you?"

"No, not anymore," he said.

His voice stayed strong, but his gaze slipped from her eyes to the place setting in front of him as he shifted in his seat.

"Divorced?"

An uncomfortable feeling started to wash over him. This was the first time since he became a widower that he actually had to say it aloud.

"No, my wife, Donna died five years ago."

"Oh Tom, I am sorry."

"Thank you, she was a wonderful woman. I would have moved heaven and earth for her," he said as his mind traveled back into his memories of his now deceased wife.

Although Kari was interested in hearing more, she started to wonder if maybe he was still in love with his long departed wife. Her vision of starting a relationship with this wonderful man may not be in her future after all. With her heart slowly sinking at the loss of a good man, before there was even a chance for a relationship to start, she decided to dive right into it and actually find out if there was any chance a bond could begin between them.

"May I ask, what happened?"

He looked up and for a brief moment, he felt tightness in his chest. He hadn't planned on bringing up his marriage, let alone the death of his wife. But, his feet were already wet in the pool, so why not plunge all the way in. He didn't even try to soften the blow, he just blurted out in a dreary tone,

"Cancer happened. It was very hard to watch a once healthy, energetic and an extremely comical spirit, become withered and incapacitated. To see Donna deteriorate before my eyes had been the hardest thing I ever had to do in my entire life."

Not sure how to respond to his obvious heartbreak, Kari felt compelled to just offer a shoulder for him to lean on.

"I am so sorry Tom; I know that must have been a horrible time."

Suddenly, something snapped in his head. He realized that this was neither the time nor the place to have this conversation. He certainly did not want to unload his entire pathetic life's story on their first date. Shifting in his seat, he straightened his back then managed to produce his award-winning smile, as he said,

"Yes, it was a bad time, but I have had enough time to grieve my wife's death and I know it is time to let her go. I want to be honest with you, if I may."

"Sure, honesty is always the best policy. What do you need to be honest about?"

"Well, you now know that my wife died five years ago, and I don't want to bore you with all the details, but what I'd like to say is this; I haven't been out with any other women since I met my Donna — way back when.

I met her, fell in love with her, married her, watched her die, and buried her. That was the worst day of my life. I believed that on the day I buried her, I would walk this miserable earth alone until, I too succumbed to death. Then... I met you. You have awoken something inside me that I cannot explain, and I really don't want to either. Since I met you last night, I have not been able to get you off my mind. The feelings and thoughts that run through my head are amazing, and I will admit, they frighten me a little too.

Now I don't want to scare you off, I just feel I have to explain that I haven't dated anyone — other than Donna, and I just may suck at it. You know, like now — how I am rambling on like a loosed lip fool, tripping over myself. How I'm trying not to be an idiot and actually accomplishing the very thing I was trying to avoid."

Looking across the table, he gazed into her eyes trying to determine if she wanted to bolt from the restaurant and possibly never see him again. However, what he did see, was an attractive woman that had an enormous amount of compassion that was just spewing from her. Even though he may have felt like an idiot, carrying on the way he did, he felt confident that he didn't show it.

Kari, on the other hand, had never felt more comfortable in her life. Just listening to him trying to explain his desires and his fears, made her want him even more.

"I am delighted and honored that you are being so honest and open with me. I too feel that I should be honest with you. I have not dated in years either and even though I have never been married, I never would have thought I would ever have a relationship. In fact, to be completely honest with you, I never would have thought anyone would be interested in me, at least not since Alan."

"Alan?"

"Yeah, Alan and I were childhood sweethearts. It started in the sixth grade all the way through high school and midway into our sophomore year of college. We were perfect together. He completed me and I him. Know what I mean? He was the true epitome of the perfect soul mate. I loved him with every ounce of my being and I knew that he loved me as much too."

Pausing, Kari was trying to decide on how to approach the topic of Alan. It had been years since she had allowed herself to even remotely poke at those painful memories of her lost love — memories that she had buried so long ago. She didn't want to bring the mood down between them, by reawakening the beast of mourning. After taking a few moments pause, she decided to just take her chances and plunge right into it.

"It was summer break and we were both home from college when he asked me to meet him down by the lake. We had a secret meeting place that was secluded and pretty well hidden from anyone passing by. I knew what he was planning to do, but I never let on that I knew. I had gotten all dressed up in my sexiest outfit, told my mother that I was heading out to meet up with Alan and off to the lake I went.

I sat by the water waiting for him to sneak up behind me and smother me with kisses. I waited, and waited, and waited some more, when finally a horrible feeling came over me. I knew that something was seriously wrong because, Alan would never forget to come get me, especially if we were meeting at the lake.

I ran home as quick as I could, hoping that he was waiting at my house. I thought maybe I misunderstood him and he wanted to pick me up to take me to the lake himself. But, then I figured if he wasn't at my house, I'd just run over to him. After all, he did live right behind my mom's house.

As I approached my house, my mother was on the porch and she had the most horrible look on her face. I immediately knew something bad had to have happened, but I never expected in a million years to hear what my mother was about to tell me. It all seemed to be in slow motion, even years after the fact. My mother stepped off the porch and started running towards me. I could see that her face was wet with tears, and her black mascara streaked her cheeks. My mind was in overdrive by now, trying to figure out what in the world had happened to get my mother so upset. Instantly I thought of my Aunt Gert. Seeing my mother so upset, I naturally assumed that she must have died. I quickened my pace and met my mother on the edge of the neighbors' front lawn. She wrapped her arms around me immediately and began to sob harder. I barely remember asking her what was wrong when, I looked between the houses and seen the flashing lights of several emergency vehicles in front of Alan's home. I tried to push my mother away from me so that I could go over there and see what was going on, but she wouldn't let me go."

Kari's throat began to seize. The words were becoming to be too difficult to say. She knew what was happening; her tears were going to start rolling down her cheeks. Even though she didn't want to go there, her feelings were like a runaway freight train, rolling downhill with no emergency stop in sight. She knew there was absolutely nothing she could do to stop it; all she could do was pray that she would be able to get through it. She was hoping against hope that their wonderful evening's mood wouldn't be ruined.

Reaching out for her glass of wine, Kari took a sip. She managed to get it down her throat, but it took some effort. The pinching feeling was returning and she wasn't too sure if she would be able to continue. Glancing from her glass to Tom's face, a calmness came over her. His gentle eyes offered her compassion and knowing that he suffered a great loss too, she managed to hold her tears at bay and summon the strength to continue. With her voice on the verge of quivering and a lump the size of a coconut in her throat, she went on.

"It seemed like an eternity, but finally my mother managed to blurt out that Alan had been in an awful accident. He was backing his car down the driveway when he remembered something that he forgot in the garage. He pulled back up the driveway and jumped out of the car, leaving it still running, as he entered the garage. Just as he was about to turn back and leave, his car began to idle high, popped out of park, slipped into drive and pinned him against the back wall of the garage. The force was so great that, it severed him in half.

I was absolutely, mortified, because I knew what Alan went in there for; he was planning to surprise me, but as I said earlier, I knew him as well as he knew himself. He hid my engagement ring in the garage and that's what he went back in there to get. They only found this out after they took his body to the morgue. The coroner had to pry open his cold, dead fingers and in his clenched hand he found the ring. His mother, bless her soul, wanted me to keep it, but I just couldn't. At the funeral home, his family allowed me five minutes alone with him, you know, so I could say good-bye. And as I paid my last respects to him, I slipped the ring off my finger and slid it into the left breast pocket of his suit. I told him to keep my love in his heart — forever."

I had never met anyone that could live up to the standards of Alan, and I guess that I am partially to blame for that too. I have found a multitude of excuses to bury myself in my work and devote every waking moment to the elderly people under my care. Sometimes it feels like I am searching for something through the stories that they tell, but I just can't put my finger on what that something could be."

Feeling a lump beginning to build in her throat for a second time, Kari decided to take another sip of her wine. Praying that she could just swallow the lump away, fortunately for her, it worked.

"On a happier note," she continued, "I found that meeting you last night was one of the better chapters in my life so far, and yes, I too am a bit scared. With that being said, maybe we both can just take this one-step at a time. You know, let's just get to know each other slowly and see what might happen. Right now, I am in no hurry to jump from the frying pan and into the fire, but I also don't want to stop seeing you. You too have tapped into something within me, although I am not sure how to take that. I just know that right now I don't want it to end. I think that for a long time, I may have been dead inside, but in less than twenty-four hours, you have managed to ignite a spark within me that I can't remember feeling. And with that, you have granted me a new beginning."

When she was finished speaking, it was her turn to search his face to see if there were signs of him wanting to escape. But what she found was, a handsome man staring back at her with a warm smile across his lips and the most beautiful soft and inviting eyes, fixated directly onto hers.

"Was that too much honesty, Tom?" she asked.

"No, not at all," he chuckled. "At least I know that we are both on the same page and I am really glad that we are."

Kari's smile broadened as she said, "Me too."

Throughout dinner, the two chatted endlessly about some of the stories that were headlining in the news. How the city officials have been crying for more taxes and how much the terrain has changed over the years. They even dabbled a little into each other's personal lives. Just two individuals, enjoying each other's company hoping to lay the foundation of a relationship on which they can build upon.

Kari was on cloud nine. Several times throughout their conversation she felt a rush of heat wash over her. At first, she thought that maybe it was the wine, but she soon realized what it really was. She was sexually aroused and her desire for him was soon approaching a critical point. If they weren't actually in a restaurant having dinner, there was no telling what she would have done.

As she looked down into her plate, a vision ran through her mind. The two of them, still at the restaurant eating dinner, she stands up, pulls the table cloth off the table, knocking everything onto the floor. She grabs Tom by the lapels of his jacket and rips his suit coat off. Then she tears the shirt off his chest. He in turn, slips his hands under her blouse and pulls it over her head. Slipping his hands into the waistband of her skirt, he slides it downward and lets it fall to the floor. Gently, he lays her onto their table then proceeds to make love to her, right there in front of all the other patrons who are eating dinner in the room.

Giggling softly to herself, that wonderful warm flush feeling ran through her body like a lightning bolt. It was a feeling that she didn't want to go away. Lost in her fantasy, she was suddenly startled back into reality when she heard,

"What's so funny?"

Snapping her head up, she found Tom had been watching her. Now she was truly embarrassed. The illicit thoughts running through her mind made her blush. There was no way in hell she

ECHOES OF THE PAST

could share those thoughts with him, but she knew she had to say something.

"Oh nothing," she said, as she started playing with the food on her plate. She was trying to buy some time to figure out what she was going tell him.

"I was just thinking about how cute it was, you know... our coming out conversation."

"What do you mean?" he asked

"Well, I know you were uncomfortable when you first started talking to me and to tell you the truth, I was nervous too. Then all of a sudden, something inside of me just relaxed. I mean, it was as if someone switched off the fear button and it was like...we could say anything to each other without being afraid. Do you know what I mean?"

It didn't take him but a minute to understand what she meant.

"Yeah, I actually do. You know, I like having that fear button switched off, it sure makes things a lot more fun and relaxing."

"It sure does," she said.

Whew, that was a close-call missy. Almost getting caught, red handed, having a dirty fantasy. Knock off the daydreams until later, when you are alone. Then you can let the fantasies really begin, she thought to herself.

Not really sure what was going on in her head, Tom knew deep down that the lame excuse she had just given him was not a truthful one. He only hoped that by the way she was smiling when it happened, it was something good. And it had something to do with the two of them.

He believed that tonight was going to be a tough night for him, being that it was his first actual date since his wife died that is. He planned to remain focused on their conversation and see how the evening played out. What he didn't expect was, actually having a great time. He honestly did not want this night to end, at least not for a while. Essentially he was having a wonderful time and found that his date was not only interesting to be with, she was also a very beautiful person—inside and out. He thought that Donna would approve too, and that feeling warmed his heart.

CHAPTER 31

Tom pulled his car into her driveway and cut the engine. The moon shone brightly in the clear night sky, as the two just sat in the quiet. A warm breeze whispered through the open windows, gently tossing little wisps of their hair atop their heads. It seemed to be an awkward moment as neither of them spoke. Two grown adults who had spent so much time together in such a short period, suddenly were at a loss of what to say or do next.

Kari, who had been ready to jump this man's bones from the first time she met him, was suddenly shy and nervous to take the plunge to the next level.

Tom on the other hand, wanted to hold back and let the moment build up until neither one of them could stop the inevitable train from its certain path.

As the two sat quietly, Tom gently slipped his arm up over the back of the seat and eventually around her shoulder. He pulled her to him so she could rest her head on his chest, then he said,

"Thank you Kari for an absolutely remarkable evening."

"Thank you too, Tom. I had an amazing time tonight."

With that, Tom leaned down and ever so gently kissed to top of her forehead as he pulled her in a little closer, to give her a hug.

Feeling his warm soft lips on her skin, she closed her eyes and just absorbed that moment in time. When he pulled back, she turned her face up to his, longing for more. Not wanting to wait for him to kiss her, she took the lead and placed her yearning lips onto his.

Tom's body was ready and willing to take this new relationship to the ultimate level, but his mind did not want to go there yet. He knew that it was always best to let that heated moment build, just like a volcano. It was always best to wait for the heat to become too hot to bear, then let the lava flow. It may have been a while since he experienced that feeling, but it is definitely not a feeling that he could forget.

Her lips were like rose petals and her skin like silk. An array of emotions and feelings began to run through him. Suddenly he found that he was having a hard time fighting back his imaginary volcano and the bulging flow of lava that was ready to burst from it. He could tell by the way that she was kissing him that, she too was ready to break the dam wide-open, but he was apprehensive about advancing any further.

He felt her hand slip down to his crotch. His natural instinct was to shift his hips up and press his now rock hard cock, into her palm. She did what came natural to her as well — she gently gripped him, full in her hand, and gently squeezed. This sent a sensation through him that he hadn't felt in a very, very long time. His voice immediately dropped a few octaves, as he moaned into her ear. He absolutely wanted her. Hearing the sound of his deep moan had sent Kari to the moon. The butterflies in her gut that were once quiet, had begun to stir again. At first, there was just a ping or two against her stomach wall, but now, a full fledge riot was taking place in there.

Managing to maneuver his free hand, Tom slipped it under her blouse and cupped one of her breasts. As he began fondling her, she too began to moan. Her body movements were sending all kinds of green light messages to him. He pressed into her, and kissed her harder as he squeezed her breast a little more firmly. Getting the message that he was sending, she squeezed him back with just a little more force than before. Just as the two seemed to be rocking to the same tune, Kari wanted him come inside so they could finish their dance when, her neighbor had turned on her porch light as she opened her front door.

Noticing at once that the darkness in the car was gone and it was replaced with an ominous light. Kari pulled back quickly and began pulling her blouse down. Shifting in his seat, Tom tried, unsuccessfully, to adjust his rock hard manhood in his pants. The pair acted just like a couple of teenagers busted by the cops for parking and making out. Then they heard a small voice call out.

"Kari, is that you?"

Terribly embarrassed, Kari replied nervously,

"Yes Mrs. Deawood, it's me."

"Are you alright dear?"

"Yes ma'am, I'm fine, thank you. You can go back inside now

Mrs. Deawood, I was just saying good night to my friend."

"Oh, I'm sorry dear; I didn't mean to interrupt anything. I'll just go back inside and the two of you can carry on."

Slipping back into her home and with full knowledge of what they were doing, Mrs. Deawood wondered why they were doing it in the driveway and not in the house, behind closed doors.

Once they heard the old woman's door close, the mood was shattered. Kari was embarrassed and Tom's, once rock-hard rock star had withered into nothingness. After a few awkward and quiet moments, the two began laughing uncontrollably.

"Oh my goodness, can you believe we just got busted by an eighty-two year old?" Kari said.

"I felt like I was sixteen and the cops were beating on my window, asking my date if she was OK."

"I know — how embarrassing. What am I going to tell that woman the next time she catches me cleaning up the yard?" she laughed.

"Just tell her the truth. At her age, I'm sure she has been around the block a few times and who knows, maybe she just might like to hear about it. I know a few dirty little old ladies myself you know."

"Oh, you do? And who might they be?"

At that moment, he leaned over and kissed her long and hard. Wrapping both arms around her, he caressed her furiously. He felt her melt into his embrace and for just a brief moment, the two felt like one. Neither of them knew it, but each of them felt it.

"I'll tell you at a later date," he whispered in her ear. "This way I know that you'll see me again."

"Alright, I'll see you again. As long as you promise we'll have just as good of a time as we did tonight."

"*That* my dear, is a promise."

Kari leaned towards him to kiss one more time. As she opened the car door to get out, she took a quick moment to adjust her clothing. She wanted to make sure that her neighbor wouldn't see anything inappropriate—it would be tough to explain how she ended up having a wardrobe malfunction.

"Thanks again Tom, it truly was an extraordinary evening."

"That Kari, is an understatement — in every sense of the word," he laughed. Then he asked, "Can I call you tomorrow?"

"No.... but you can meet me at the library if you'd like. I planned on being there when it opens."

"The library it is then. I'll see you in the morning."

Slipping out of his car, Kari headed up the driveway to her front door. Once she was safely on her porch and out of view of Mrs. Daewood, she turned to blow Tom a kiss.

As his taillights diminished into the darkness, Kari entered the house and locked the door behind her.

CHAPTER 32

The evening's events were already replaying in her mind, as she was waiting for the tub to fill. She wanted to soak in a hot tub before going to bed, hoping that the warm water would help soothe her into a more restful sleep.

Removing all of her clothing, she stood naked in front of the mirror. Looking at her body with a keen eye, she wanted to see what she really looked like, before allowing Tom to see her that is. She was aware that she was not one of those young, beautiful, thin girls, but she wasn't in too bad of shape either — for her age. A little love handle here and there, maybe a small muffin cap behind her armpits, and OK, maybe her breasts were sagging a little — nothing like the force of gravity bringing things down, but all in all, she looked pretty good.

She ran her hands along her body, feeling the smoothness of her skin and the contours of her shape. Feeling her waist dip in and hips mildly curve out. Then she slowly guided her hands upward. Once she got to her breasts and cupped them into her hands, a shockwave of excitement surged through her body. A feeling she hadn't experienced in a lot of years, but certainly not one she had ever forgotten.

She climbed into the bathtub and submerged herself into the warm water. Once she laid back, she let her mind and her hands wander. Her mind replayed the moment Tom had slipped his hand under her blouse. She wanted him to find her breast so badly and the moment he did, her insides were bursting with excitement. It felt like a million fireworks began exploding, all at the same time. As her mind replayed the events, her hands were traveling along her wanting body. She consciously slid one hand up to her breast where she began caressing and squeezing her nipple, while her other hand quietly slipped beneath the water. Slowly, she guided her hand down her belly, around her hip and across her thigh, until it found the aching and longing spot between her legs. Her fingers knew what her body ached for and in the heat of the moment, nothing was going to stop that from happening. She hadn't pleasured herself in a long time and obviously, it had been long overdue. She must have orgasmed more than a dozen times while she soaked in the tub because, by the time she came around to opening her eyes, her hands and feet had become prunes.

Dropping the large plush towel on the floor after drying herself off, Kari walked naked to her bedroom. She headed for her dresser to grab a nightgown, but instead of slipping it on she decided to do something she had never done before — sleep in the nude.

The feeling of the sheets against her bare body and the cool evening breeze that gently flowed over her damp skin had quickly aroused her. Except this time, she wished that Tom was there to satisfy her.

As the sun began to rise, she quickly got out of bed and dressed for the day. She could hardly wait for the library to open. She began to wonder if her desire for going to the library was for her research or if it was because Tom would be there.

Maybe I'll tell him about Tess and see if he might like to help me find out more about her, she thought. A smile formed across her lips as the thought of the two of them working together on her project, had crossed her mind.

She found herself checking the clock several times, but every time she looked, only a minute or two had passed.

"Man, it's like time is standing still. I can't believe I still have two hours before it opens," she said to herself.

"What am I going to do for two hours?"

Sitting on the end of her couch was her laptop. It seemed to be beckoning her begging her to turn it on. She decided to begin searching for anything on the old prison, that surely will help to pass the time and if she's lucky, she might even find some useful information out too.

As she began plugging some key words into her search engine, lists of URL'S began popping up. But, as she scrolled thru them, she found she couldn't concentrate. She began to think of Tom again, found herself wondering what he was doing. At the mere thought of him, a warm flush feeling began to rise up inside her once more, but this time; she decided to shake the thoughts from her head and forced herself to concentrate on her research.

CHAPTER 33

Clara arrived a few minutes earlier than usual to open up the library. As she pulled her car into the lot, she had seen that there was an early customer waiting for her to open the doors.

As she climbed the steps to the front door, she heard footsteps behind her. Although the area is a reasonably safe neighborhood, one couldn't be too careful. Slowly she slipped her hand into her bag to grab her can of mace when a voice called out behind her.

"Good morning Clara."

Stopping dead in her tracks, a sense of relief soon washed over her. She was more than happy when she realized she recognized the voice. Releasing her grip on the can of mace, she turned around and said,

"Well, good morning Kari, what brings you down to the library so early?"

"I was hoping to get an early start on some further research. It's a bit more difficult to do during the work week, especially on the days I get off late."

"Yes, I'm sure it is. Come on in. I'll make a fresh pot of coffee and you can get started on your work."

"That sounds fabulous, thanks."

The two entered the building and while Clara headed to the kitchen to make the coffee, Kari headed off to the basement.

While waiting for Clara and the coffee, she started up the microfilm machine and began scrolling through some of the old news articles. Page after page, article after article, nothing new was coming up about Tess. She had gone through one entire roll of film and began loading another one when, she heard Clara coming down the steps.

"Kari, I got your fresh hot coffee here," Clara quietly said.

"Oh, thank you. It smells so good."

"Yeah, it does. I hope you like your coffee on the strong side, because this is Columbian."

She handed Kari a cup and was just about to leave when, something on the microfilm screen caught her eye.

"You're digging into the old prison, right?"

"Yes. I'm trying to see if I can confirm a story I heard. Why?"

"Well, I probably shouldn't tell you about this but, I have a very interesting little locked room just full of old paperwork."

"What do you mean?"

"Come on, follow me."

Clara led Kari to the dark side of the basement. Along the far corner of the room, there was a door. Clara pulled out her key ring and without much hesitation; she selected a key that unlocked the door.

As they stepped inside, the smell of old, musty paper and decaying cardboard greeted them. Clara turned the light on, which revealed a small room neatly stockpiled with boxes stacked against the far back wall.

"What is all this?" Kari asked.

"I guess you could say that *this* is a treasure trove, just for you."

"What are you talking about Clara? You aren't making any sense."

Clara walked deeper into the room and grabbed one of the boxes. She set it down on the single wooden desk that was in the center of the room and open it.

"These boxes have been in here for more than sixty years and they are filled with old files from the prison. I believe that when they shut it down and started pulling everything out, they didn't have any place to store them. The old city council members must have decided to keep the boxes locked up down here until they could find a better location, but as time went on, you know, people forget, others die and voilà! Forgotten paperwork left behind, just for the pickings."

"Are you kidding me?" Kari was in total disbelief.

"No, I'm not kidding you Kari. One rule though, you cannot take anything out of this room. I probably shouldn't have even shown any of this to you, but I figure that most, if not all of these people are probably dead by now. And, who is going to know, let alone care — right?

All I know is, the State never came back to get this stuff and the city council that we have right now, more than likely, doesn't even know this stuff exists. Hell, the only reason why I know about it is because, the very first day I was to open the library alone, I found that one of the keys on my ring unlocked the door. I had been curious for years as to what could be behind this locked door. In fact, when I first started working here, I had asked the old head librarian about it. She had gotten very angry with me and insisted that no one was ever to enter this room. She informed me, that one day someone of authority would arrive to empty the contents out of the room.

Well, as of right now, nobody has ever shown up. In fact, no one has ever mentioned anything about it in years. I believe that all this stuff has just simply slipped their minds."

Looking over to Kari, then around the room, she continued,
"Go ahead and sift through these old boxes. If you find something that helps you with your search, let me know and I will see if I can get a copy for you. But please, promise me you won't let anyone else know about this stuff. I don't want to lose my job over this, you know, just in case there does happen to be one old coot still roaming around out there that does remember these files are still here."

"I promise Clara. Wow, I just cannot believe that they left all this behind. Thank you so much, this should make my research a lot easier — I hope."

Slipping out of the room, Clara headed back upstairs, leaving Kari alone to rummage through the rotting boxes of old prison documents.

Opening the first box, Kari inspected each document carefully. It didn't take her long to figure out what all the forms had in common either, each one had been stamped with a single word — *Released.* At least now, she felt that she was finally looking in the right place. By Veeona's version of events, she knew the State had released the majority of the women back into society and that included Tess. Somewhere in one of the many boxes stacked in this secret room, was information about Tess's arrest.

Kari had been so absorbed with her search, that as she sifted through the boxes she had lost track of time. She had been completely engrossed in reading the old records that, she had forgotten Tom was supposed to meet up with her there. As she began to open another box, she heard a voice calling out,

"Kari? Are you down here?"

She froze at the sound that broke the dead silence in the room. It took her a few moments to comprehend what she just heard, when the faint voice called out to her once more.

"Kari, where are you?" she heard. "Are you down here?"

Scrambling to close up the box, Kari slipped out of the room, silently closing the door behind her. As she slowly emerged from the dark shadowy corner at the back of the basement, she made it appear as if she was searching the last row of shelves of books for a something specific.

"Here I am Tom," she said as she made her way back towards the microfilm machine.

"I'm sorry that I'm so late," he said, "I just couldn't wake up this morning and when I finally did, I had a phone call from my grandfather. I had to go over there and help him out."

"Oh, what happened?"

"He fell. I thought that I would have to either call for an ambulance or take him to the hospital, but by the time I got there and checked him out, he was fine. Thank God."

"That's good."

Finding herself now torn between Tom staying with her or secretly wishing he would leave, Kari was in a bit of a quandary. Although she was happy that he was there, her new treasure trove of endless information was all-consuming for her. Tom had sensed that something was a bit off with Kari but, not certain what it could be. He then asked,

"Kari, are you alright?"

"Yeah, sure I am. Why, what's the matter?"

"You just seem … distant."

Feeling like a deer caught in headlights, Kari knew that she was no good at lying and besides, she thought, *what harm would there be in telling him about the locked room and let him read some of the old prison records too. I'm sure Clara wouldn't mind, after all, she knows Tom wouldn't blab to anyone about it.*

Apologizing for her odd behavior, and before she could talk herself out of it, she blurted,

"I found something."

"Oh? Does it have to do with your friend, Tess?"

"Yes," she exclaimed, barely able to conceal her excitement.

"So … are you going to tell me about it or do I have to try and guess what it is that you found?"

"Well, I'm not sure I can tell you."

"Huh? Let me get this straight. First, you tell me you that found something, and then you tell me that you can't tell me what you found. Did I miss something here, or …?"

"No, I know it sounds weird, but I can explain."

"Please do. I'm all ears right about now," he smiled.

"Well, when I got to the library this morning, Clara brought me down here to show me something. She told me about a locked room that she had found years ago. It had been off limits to her until she took over as the head librarian. When she took over some years ago, she entered the room to find out what was so *top secret* about it. She found the room filled with boxes of some old records. She made me promise not to let anyone else know about the room or its contents, because she's afraid that she might lose her job over it."

"Is this your version of not telling me then?" he mused.

Realizing she inadvertently did exactly what Clara asked her not to do, she decided to spill the beans in its entirety.

"I want to show you something Tom, but you have to promise me that you will never speak of this with anyone other than me."

With his interest peaked, he made an invisible X with his index finger across his heart as he said, "I promise — cross my heart."

Convinced that he was being truthful, she grabbed his hand and led him into the dark shadowy corner of the basement. Once they were both inside and door firmly closed, she turned on the light to reveal boxes upon boxes, neatly stacked against the far wall — four rows deep.

Tom's eyes surveyed the room, trying to take it all in. He felt a bit confused when he finally asked,

"What is this all about Kari?"

She walked over to the desk where the box was, the one that she had been searching through when Tom had showed up and said,

"Inside these boxes are all the records from the old prison. It has all of the inmate's information, files on the prison guards and possibly information on that bastard of a warden too."

Tom's eyes grew large and his jaw dropped, complete shock came over his face.

"You can't be serious," he said in utter disbelief.

"As serious as a heart attack," she said.

"Oh my lord, there must be tons of information in here. We might even be able to find out what actually happened to the warden. Hell, we might even find out who really killed him."

Standing in awe, Tom stared at all the boxes in the room. He then raised both his hands and ran his fingers through his hair, as he let out a deep breathy sigh.

"Look at all this. Where do you begin?" he asked.

"I know. I was just as overwhelmed as you are right now when I first came in here. Clara just grabbed a box, set it on this desk and told me to start digging in — one box at a time. I had only gotten through two boxes and just started on my third, when you came down. Now that there are two of us, things should go a little faster — of course, if you are interested in helping me."

"I'd love to. Are you sure you want me to help you?"

"Well, how about you grab a box and start going through it over there and I'll just continue to work on this one."

"I'll take that as a yes."

Taking off his jacket, Tom rolled up his sleeves and proceeded to open his first box.

CHAPTER 34

The two had been at it for hours, going through box after box. Neither one of them had found any valuable information that would help Kari's research advance forward. Suddenly a large gurgling sound broke the silence in the room.

"What in heaven's name was that?" Kari cried out.

Looking over at Tom, who was just closing up yet another box of useless information, she had seen a small smile form across his lips.

"That, my dear, is my internal alarm clock."

"What? What are you talking about?"

Glancing at his watch, he said,

"Do you realize that we have been down here for four hours? I think we need to take a break and have some lunch. My stomach is telling me it is time to eat."

Kari had no idea that they had been at it for that long and without hesitation, she grabbed all the papers that she had carefully taken out of the box and haphazardly threw them back in. She then closed the box up and stacked it with the group of boxes they had already searched.

"I'm ready when you are," she said. "But, I think I'll come back later and look through a couple more boxes this evening."

The two quickly and quietly closed the door to the secret room and like stealth ninja warriors; they snuck out of the dark shadows of the basement, making sure none of the other people in the basement would notice them.

When they reached the main level of the library, Tom slipped out the door to get the car. Kari on the other hand, immediately sought out Clara to inform her she was done for a while and that she would be back after lunch.

As Tom waited for her to emerge from the building, he felt like a young schoolboy waiting to go on his first date. His nervousness and excitement was completely out of character and he wasn't quite sure if he was delighted or frightened by it. But, the moment he had seen her walk down the steps and get into his car, he pushed all his fickle feelings away and asked,

"What do you feel like for lunch?" she asked.

"To tell you the truth, I really hadn't thought about it," he said.

"Well, if it wasn't for your stomach growling, I wouldn't have known it was lunch time at all."

"Well, good thing it rumbled then." A smile quickly lit up his face as he put the car into gear and it remained there as he pulled out of the parking lot.

"Where are you taking me?" she asked.

"Well, I thought maybe we could just grab a sandwich. Then I thought about taking you over to the park where we could eat down by the riverbank. What do you think of that?"

"Sounds like fun — let's do it!"

Tom drove down to his favorite coffee shop and went inside to get their lunches. When he came out, he was carrying a large grocery bag in one hand and balancing two cups of coffee in the other. Kari watched his balancing act, keeping a careful eye on him. As he got closer to the car, she immediately got out to help him by taking the coffees out of his hand.

"Thank you. I wasn't sure I was going to make it all the way here without dropping something" he chuckled.

"I know. I was watching you as you came out. I must say though, you are pretty good at balancing things, aren't you."

Flashing his beautiful smile again, he put the car in gear and headed to a secluded park that he had always like going to. It was a nice quiet place where the two could be alone. They could have their lunch sitting on the riverbank and enjoy the peace and quiet of the day — together.

They drove for some thirty minutes or so, taking several dirt roads when, Kari had a feeling of déjà vu wash over her.

"Where are we going Tom?"

"You'll see. We are almost there."

Enjoying the ride, Kari couldn't help but observe and appreciate the beautiful scenery along the road. Suddenly something seemed familiar to her, but she was not able to put her finger on it.

Shooting a quick glance her way, Tom found her deep in thought.

"What's the matter?" he asked.

"This road looks familiar to me."

"Really?" he thought that was odd, because as far as he knew, no one had ever been to his grandfather's property — ever.

Making one final turn before bringing the car to a halt near an almost perfect Ebony tree, he stopped the car and then cut the engine.

"We're here," he exclaimed.

Getting out of the car Kari grabbed the coffees, while Tom snagged the large grocery bag out of the back seat. With his free hand, he laced his fingers through hers and led her down towards the river bank. He headed for a soft patch of green grass under the only tree nearest to the river, roughly three feet away from the water's edge.

As Kari surveyed the area, Tom had produced a blanket from inside the bag and laid it on top of the grass.

"Where did that come from?" she asked.

"Oh my friends at the coffee shop thought that I could use this blanket to sit on while we ate. They are always looking out for my best interest," he mused.

"I see," she said.

As they ate, Kari looked out at the river, taking in all of nature's beauty. Tom hoped she loved the spot as much as he did. He treasured going there to escape the world for a while. This was one of his secret retreats and for him to bring someone he hardly knows to a place that he reveres as a sanctuary, greatly surprised him.

With lunch out of the way, Tom once again dug into the large grocery bag. This time he brought out a chilled bottle of wine and two beautifully etched wine glasses.

"What is this?"

"I thought it would be nice to have some wine while we sit here by the water. I often come here just for the quiet and solitude. I also thought that it would be nice to be here with a beautiful woman, such as you and have a bottle of wine. Just two people enjoying the moment — together."

Looking deep into his eyes, she smiled and said,

"I'd love to have some wine with you. This place is a perfect

Tom. Thank you for sharing it with me. I can see why you would come out here. It is so…"

"Serene?"

"Yes. That is a perfect word for an absolutely perfect place. Serene!"

With the last of the wine drunk and the bottle empty, Kari was feeling the effects of the wine in her head. She felt so ready and willing to let him have his way with her, right there under the old oak tree. The thought of making love outside and in broad daylight, excited her even more. At that very moment, she was ready for anything. She silently wished that Tom would suggest that they take a dip in the river; she would have been the first one stripped of her clothing and in the river, skinny-dipping. The wine she drank turned out to be an effective aphrodisiac that heightened her sexual desires along with her prowess. Laying her head on his shoulder, she let her fantasies run wild. The butterflies in her lower belly were wildly dancing again and the heat between her legs began to rise instantaneously. What she really wanted at that precise moment was, Tom to seduce her.

With her head resting on his shoulder, Tom could smell her hair. The scent of her heightened his senses and aroused something deep within him that he hadn't thought was possible. Slipping a finger under her chin, he gently lifted her face to his. Looking deep into her eyes, he had an overwhelming desire to kiss her full on the mouth.

There they were, just two individuals, lying together under a magnificent Oak tree. Alone in a part of the world where nobody else could see them and unbeknownst to either of them, they both had lust on their minds. Following a feeling that came so naturally to him, Tom leaned in and placed his soft wet lips onto hers. Everything about that kiss screamed at him to take her. Her lips over his, her tongue darting in and around his mouth, and the taste of the wine she had just drunk, told him she was ready.

His erection was back and it was standing at full attention. Being very aware of what his body was telling him, he no longer wanted to fight off the moment. He grabbed her around her waist and pulled her toward him. He longed to feel every bit of her, pressing firmly against him. He pulled her closer still, as he passionately leaned in and kissed her, unlike any other woman he had ever kissed before.

As the passion between them grew to a tsunami level, Tom somehow managed to pull himself away from her moist and wanting lips. Surprised and very disappointed, Kari wasn't sure why he had abruptly stopped kissing her.

"What's wrong?" she asked, slightly out of breath.

"Nothing, I just don't want to rush things. I'm sorry, please don't read anything into this, I just don't want to ruin anything that we may have going for us."

Moved by his gentlemen like manners, Kari found that even though she was ready and willing, she could not help but respect his resolve. Laying back onto the blanket they both just stared upwards through the tree limbs and looked up to the sky when, Tom rose from the blanket and said,

"Come on, I want to show you something."

"What?" she asked.

"You'll see," he grabbed her hand and they headed for the car.

He drove down a small path that led deep into the woods. As the trees grew thicker, the intertwining branches began to block out the sun, and an eerie silence filled the air. Even with the noise of the car tires crunching on the dirt road, the silence was almost deafening. Gratefully, the light at the end of the path came into view. As the car approached the end of the narrowing path, Tom navigated the car around a short bend and then she saw it. A quaint little cabin came into view.

"What's this?"

"*This* is the cabin I told you about."

He pulled the car right up to the front door and slid it into Park. As they both got out Tom was fumbling for the key to the place, but Kari was more interested in the area surrounding the cabin than the cabin itself.

A hundred yards away from the cabin ran the river. The area was just as serene and beautiful as the spot where they enjoyed lunch. As she surveyed the area, she could hear the light trickle of water, like the sound of a small waterfall. She found the sound soothing and all too familiar, just like being at Aunt Gert's place. Tom, on the other hand, wanted nothing more than to get her into the cabin, but all Kari wanted to do was, walk down towards the river and see the view. Without realizing it, that was exactly what Kari set off to do.

Tom was at the cabin's door focused on trying to get the locks opened, as Kari slipped down the hill, making a B-line to the river's edge. As he finally managed to get the door unlocked, he noticed she was no longer standing behind him. Surveying the area, he found she had wandered off down to the riverbank. Seeing her standing there, he quietly headed towards her.

Standing there watching the water glide by, she felt him slip his arms around her waist where he gently leaned her back against his chest. Her insides began to quiver as she savored the moment. With his warm breath on her neck, the scent of his cologne, and his strong arms resting around her, she felt as if she had died and gone to heaven.

"What are you looking at?" he whispered with a low voice, into her ear.

"I love being near the river, always have. My Aunt had a place in the woods, similar to yours. It was near a river too, you know, for all those bonfires that I told you about the other night at dinner. Do you know what the best part that I loved the most about being out there was? It was listening to the sound the water made, as it flowed on by. As I stand here, I can almost smell the wood burning from the bonfire. This is a magnificent place Tom; you should consider yourself extremely lucky to have it."

A warm breath followed by soft, moist lips greeted her neck, as Tom leaned in to kiss her. Cuddled up in each other's arms, they just sat on the riverbank watching the water flow downstream. The pair spent the afternoon taking in the view while basking in the sun's warm rays — just enjoying each other's company.

CHAPTER 35

Having to check on his ailing grandfather, Tom reluctantly dropped Kari off at the library. As he pulled the car up to the sidewalk closest to the library's entrance, he pulled Kari towards him and kissed her one last time. It was a kiss like no other, as if he were a sailor leaving port for a six-month tour of duty. Kari melted in his embrace as she kissed him back with just as much passion. Half-heartedly, she opened the car door and stepped out onto the sidewalk, when she heard him say,

"I'm sorry I can't join you in there, but can we talk later?"

"Hey, don't be sorry Tom, your grandfather's health comes first, and yeah, if you have the time later, give me a call."

After reassuring him that everything was fine, she closed the car door and headed up the steps to the library's entrance.

In the library, Kari found Clara perched behind the checkout desk, right where she was when she left for lunch. As she reached the desk, she asked Clara for permission to re-enter the secret room so that could resume her tedious task of searching through all those boxes.

"That was a pretty long lunch Kari. Did you two have fun?" she winked.

"Clara! Honestly, what kind of a woman do you think I am?" she smiled.

"I think you're like the rest of us women in this town. Hot to trot for Mister Handsome and Available. I've known Tom for years and I can tell you this; he hasn't so much as cast an eye on any woman, especially since his wife died."

"Yes, he told me about her. That was a heartbreaking story."

"Yeah, it was. But it's been a while, you know. He should be seeing other women by now and I noticed that he seems to be interested in a certain someone who happens to be standing right in front of me."

Feeling a bit embarrassed, Kari could feel a wave of heat rush over her cheeks.

"Now don't bother blushing honey, just about every woman in this town and probably the next two over, have tried their best to catch him. He is undeniably someone worth catching. He is very easy on the eyes — if you know what I mean. Not to mention his sparkling personality and he definitely has enough money in the bank to satisfy even the most pampered woman in the Hamptons. You snag him, Kari, and you'll have hit a grand slam. And you want to know what's even better? It will be easy for you to do it too, because he seems to be really into you."

"Clara, stop it now. I just met the man. So what if we had dinner last night and lunch today. That doesn't mean a thing."

"Really Kari? I'll have you know, I am a librarian — not an idiot. I see how he's falling all over you. He brought in two coffees and a bag of bagels for you this morning."

"He did not bring me a bagel…. it was a muffin," she offered lightly.

"A MUFFIN! Excuse me for not having x-ray vision through a paper bag. Kari, sweetie, Tom NEVER comes into this library with anything…. EVER! And, might I add, never has he brought anything in for anyone else before either. Now either you are playing dumb or you just really don't see it, but trust me when I say, he is smitten by you."

Hearing the words Clara was saying, coupled with the sensual afternoon she just spent with Tom, Kari thought maybe Clara might just be on to something. After all, she too felt something for Tom. Being near him moved her. He alone had managed to stir feelings and emotions that she herself thought were non-existent. Feeling content inside for the first time, she had an epiphany about herself. She isn't dead inside.

A sense of relief washed over her and her spirits rose to a level she had never reached before, not even with Alan. Maybe, just maybe, she had found someone that is into her as she is to him.

Clara came around the corner of her desk, gave Kari a gentle hug, and then handed her a single key to unlock the door to the secret room.

CHAPTER 36

Rummaging through the boxes, Kari finally found the box that contained Tess's file. As she dug through the papers, she also came across files on Vie.

Locking the door behind her, she concealed the files as best as she could, as she went in search of Clara.

"Clara," she whispered.

"Yes," a voice called back from the office behind the checkout desk.

"Can I use the copier? I think I may have found something of use."

Clara poked her head out the office door, and then quickly glanced around the library. After making sure nobody was watching, she motioned Kari to come in and join her, which was where the copier happened to be located.

"Ok, hurry up and do what you have to do. When you are done, leave the files in the bottom drawer of this desk. I'll put them away later."

"Thanks a million Clara, I owe you. Maybe on your next day off we can have lunch — my treat."

Smiling, Clara said,

"That sounds great. I'll check my schedule and let you know."

Alone in the office, Kari copied everything that was in both files. Slipping her new found information into her purse, she placed the original files into the bottom drawer of the desk just as Clara instructed, then she slipped back out into the main library.

"Are you all set Kari?" Clara asked.

"Yes, I am. Thank you for all your help."

"When do you think you will be back?"

"I'm not sure, maybe next weekend. Now don't you forget that we have a lunch date."

"I won't, but I won't see a day off until next week. I'm covering for one of the other librarians this week."

Grabbing a pen, Kari quickly jotted her phone number down a slip of paper, and handed it over to her.

"Call me when you're free. We can even do dinner if you'd like."

Waving goodbye as she thanked her again, Kari headed out of the library. She was now more than anxious to get home so that she could start reading the documents that were bulging out of her purse.

CHAPTER 37

Sitting at her kitchen table, Kari took the papers that she had copied out of her purse and placed them in a neat pile in the center of the table. Taking the top page into her hands, she began to read.

Most of the documents didn't really have the type of information that offered a glimpse into the person's life, other than the standard description of an individual. The usual information required to help identify them, if they happen to become a repeated offender. Things like: Name, Date of Birth, Height, Weight, Eye Color, etc.…

After going through just about half of the stack of papers, Kari began to think that this was going to be a huge waste of time, when she came across an arrest record. The document not only revealed a mug shot of Tess, it also described the reason for her arrest. With eyes bugged out and her jaw dropping, nearly to the floor, Kari couldn't believe what she just read. Never in a million years would she have ever believed that Tess could have committed — Murder.

Turning her attention to the remaining pile of papers on her table, she grabbed them and began hastily sifting through them, hoping to find something more. As she flipped through page after page, she found a single piece of paper that had actual handwriting on it. Not resembling any of the other forms in the pile, Kari stopped to examine that one a little more closely. Then it hit her — she was holding Tess's written confession.

Staring at it for the longest time, she was not sure if she really wanted to know all the details. She had never been faced with having a senior citizen capture her heart the way that Tess had, and then discover that they are not the person that they appear to be. She questioned her own ability to be able to carry on with Tess, if indeed she found that she was an actual murderer.

With her emotions seesawing back and forth, she was unsure if her attitude towards Tess would change once she read the document. Nevertheless, her curiosity had taken over and she decided that she needed to read it. Telling herself, the Tess that she had come to know — was no longer the woman that she had been all those years ago. Now that her conscious felt clear, Kari poured herself a glass of wine, settled in her chair and began to read Tess's confession.

I, Tesla L. Parker, was at Henry's Diner on University Rd., having dinner with a friend. It was the evening of March 3rd and we arrived at 6:00 P.M. At approximately 9:00 PM., we left the diner and went our separate ways. As I proceeded home, alone, which was roughly six blocks away, a stranger approached me and asked if I had a match to light his cigarette. I told him no, that I did not smoke and I continued on my way. He followed me for one block and as I neared the Pharmacy & Pawn Shop on Rochester Rd., the man ran up behind me, put his hand over my mouth and drug me into the alley between the two stores. I was struggling to get away because; he was dragging me to the end of the alley. He socked me in the face and I blacked out. I started to come around just as he finished raping me, when I picked up a piece of timber that was lying near me and I began to hit him over and over again. It was dark and I do not know where I hit him, but eventually he fell down. I thought I saw a shadow of another person in the alley, but I was hurt and scared. I didn't waste any time, when I saw him hit the ground I ran. I didn't stop running until I got all the way home.

The statement above is true and accurate to the best of my recollection.

Tesla L. Parker x Tesla L. Parker   Date: 3-22-47

Stunned at what she had just read, Kari was speechless.

Without even thinking, or knowing what time it was, she picked up her phone and immediately called Tom.

Ring.... ring.... .ring, she heard through her end of the phone — then,

"Hello."

"Hello—Tom, it's Kari, can you come over? I found something very interesting."

She sounded nervous, concerned, worried and excited all at the same time, perking his curiosity.

"Are you alright?" he asked.

"Yeah, sorry. I'm just blown away by what I just found. Can you come by now?"

"Sure, I'll be over in a few minutes."

A deep sense of relief washed over her, knowing there was somebody else that she could talk to about all this. She poured herself another glass of wine, took a huge sip in order to calm herself down.

Twenty minutes had passed by the time she heard a knock at the door. Knowing it had to be him; she swung the door open and pulled him inside. With a firm grip on his hand, she led him straight into the kitchen.

"Whoa, what's the rush little lady?"

"Tom, you won't believe what I just found."

"What?" he asked.

Standing next to the table that was scattered with papers, Kari picked up the handwritten confession, handed it to him and said,

"Read this. Oh my god, you are not going to believe it."

"Ok, give me a minute," he told her. "Let's see what this is all about."

As he began to read it over, Kari watched him carefully. She paid special attention to his facial expressions, in hopes that she would be able to see that *aha!* moment in his face. Much to her disappointment, she did not. In fact, when he finished reading the paper, he handed it back to her with no expression at all, then said,

"Am I missing something here? I don't know what you got out of this, but it really doesn't mean or say anything significant."

Flabbergasted by what she just heard come out of his mouth, she cried out,

"What? What do you mean this is nothing significant?"

"What do *you* think it means Kari?" he asked.

He purposely used a soothing tone of voice to try to calm her down; knowing that she wasn't thinking rationally and right now, even though he's not sure why she became all worked up over this, being rational is exactly what she needed to be.

"Hey, come on. Take a breath, it's OK," he said as he put his arm around her.

"Would you like some tea or coffee or something?"

"That my dear, sounds great." He gave her his award-winning smile and just as he hoped, her temper started to fade away.

With Kari in the kitchen making the coffee, Tom sat down and began to look over all the papers that were scattered around the table. He had found Tess's arrest record and began reading it over. When he read that she was a convicted for murder, he realized immediately why Kari had gotten so upset.

Picking up Tess's statement again, he began to re-read it. Hoping that now, it may make better sense to him. He read it for a third time, and still something just didn't seem right about it.

"Hey,' he called out, 'I think you owe me an apology."

"Apology? For what?" she shot back, as the heat of her anger wanted to return.

"I think you forgot to mention to me a little *unknown* fact like — she was in for murder!" he exclaimed.

Instantaneously, Kari's anger had completely disappeared and was immediately replaced with utter embarrassment. Silence had filled the air for several moments, when finally she heard,

"I don't hear anything?" he jovially said as he continued going over the papers on the table. Then, as if on cue, Kari uttered a meek and almost inaudible '*I'm sorry*', that floated to his ears. Smiling over his triumph, he continued surfing the remaining stack of papers. Just as he was nearing the end of the pile, he came across the arrest record for Vie.

"Hey, I just found an arrest record for someone named Vie. What does she have to do with all this?"

"Hang on a sec, I'm almost done here."

Kari brought two cups of fresh brewed coffee over to the table and sat down.

"OK, now what did you find?" she asked.

"Who is Vie and what does she have to do with Tess?"

Kari took a sip of her coffee and then proceeded to tell Tom the story that Veeona told her a couple of weeks earlier.

After Kari finished telling him what she knew, Tom was now completely enthralled by the mystery of this Tess Parker. He grabbed the written statement and looked it over yet again when suddenly, he rose from his chair and said,

"Kari, I have to go."

"What? You just got here."

"I know, but there is something that I need to check out."

Leaning over, he placed his mouth onto hers and gave her a kiss. Oh, how he ached for her touch, to feel her soft silky skin pressing against him. His body wanted to stay, but his brain was screaming at him to leave. Remarkably, he managed to pull away and make it all the way to the front door before he began to feel an erection coming on. The look on Kari's face was that of surprise, and of disappointment, but Tom knew that right now he had a hot lead he needed to follow.

CHAPTER 38

Monday morning came fast and early, like all Mondays do. Much to her dismay and for the first time ever, Kari didn't want to go to work. All she wanted to do was to continue with her investigation, but she knew that it would have to wait until the end of her shift. Tired and a little groggy, she headed off to work.

Locking her purse in her locker and stowing her key safely away, Kari headed down the hallway to room 237. As she lightly tapped on the door, it started to swing open. Stepping into the room, she found Tess sitting in her rocking chair, rocking back and forth. She crossed the room and headed towards her when, she noticed that not only was Tess dressed; she was waiting for her.

"Good morning Tess. Did you have a good weekend?"

Tess didn't move a muscle, she just rocked in her rocking chair. Surveying the room and finding nothing out of place, Kari grabbed a chair, placed it next to her charge and sat down.

Several minutes had passed with an awkward silence that filled the room. For the first time in a long time, Kari was at a loss for words. She honestly didn't know what to say, especially now that she knew some of Tess's past. All kinds of thoughts were running through her mind; *Don't give her a knife, Only plastic utensils, I've seen the scars on the ones that don't, Nothing hot to drink.* The thoughts were endless, but she just couldn't believe that this fragile old woman sitting next to her was dangerous, let alone a murderer. Shaking the thoughts from her head, she tried to be as natural as possible as she went to get the wheelchair to take Tess out for a walk.

"Come on Tess. Get in the wheelchair and let's take a walk."

Without much hesitation, Tess got into the wheelchair. As they were leaving the room, Tess grabbed her hat off the table and slipped it onto her head. This brought a huge smile to Kari's face and any reservations that she had when she first arrived this morning, were long gone now.

Pushing her down the path that they had taken so many times before, Kari brought Tess out to the flower garden that they had been working on. As they got closer, Kari was utterly surprised that the garden was completed. Someone had removed all the remaining weeds, pulled out all the old gnarled roots and even added new top soil.

Planted in the new dirt were, hostas, chrysanthemums, african daisies, pansies, gardenias, and in the center, a beautiful hydrangea plant. All with blooms ready to burst open and expose an array of beautiful colors, just like the soft pastel hues in a rainbow.

"Oh my gosh! Tess, who did all of this?"

Her question met only by silence.

As she walked around the flower bed, admiring all the beautiful foliage and plants, Kari was undeniably astounded.

"This is absolutely, beautiful," she announced with such pride in her voice.

Knowing there would be no response from Tess, that didn't stop her from continuing to ask questions. It was more for her own sake that she continued to talk. As if by speaking her questions aloud, it would help her to ascertain the answers that she so desperately sought.

After she walked around the garden for a second time, she noticed a pair of yard gloves tucked in between the spokes of Tess's wheelchair. She bent down and retrieved the gloves from the spokes, and that's when she noticed how dirty they were.

"So, you were busy this weekend, weren't you?"

Smiling down at her, she then asked,

"How Tess? Who helped you do all this?"

Tess offered nothing verbally, but her eyes seemed to be smiling, maybe even laughing at her.

With the secret safely stuck inside a woman that refused to speak, Kari leaned towards her and kissed her on her cheek.

"That was for all your hard work. I don't know who helped you, but I'm glad you did it. You did a remarkable job and I'm sure once all these flowers bloom, this flowerbed will be even more beautiful."

CHAPTER 39

Lying in bed, with eyes wide open, Kari could hardly believe that the week had gone by so quickly. Another weekend already upon her and she could hardly wait for the day to begin.

Throwing off the covers and bouncing out of bed, she quickly dressed and soon was heading out the door. Today was the day that she hoped to get the answers to some, if not all, of her questions about Tess. Just as she opened the front door, she was more than happy to see Tom standing on her porch.
"Well hello there," she said.
"Good morning gorgeous, did you have a good night's sleep?"
"As a matter of fact, I did. What brings you out so early?"
"Can I come in?"
By the look on his face, Kari could tell that something was troubling him. She was unsure if she should be alarmed or not, when she said,
"Sure, come on in. What's the matter? Is your grandfather OK?"
"Yes, he's fine."
Taking her hand, he led her to the table where he asked her to sit down.

Nervousness started to set in, as she wondered what was wrong. What had him so obviously distraught? Kari didn't like not knowing what was going on and that was when she felt her heart had begun to pound in her chest. For a moment, all she could hear was the sound of her own heartbeat and it was deafening.
Allowing Tom to guide her to the nearest chair, she hesitantly sat down. Tom stood before her for a moment, staring directly into her eyes, when he finally sat in the chair next to her. Kari never took her eyes off him; she tried to read his face. Her eyes followed the contour lines on his brow, and then slowly down to the creases around his eyes. She noticed the smoothness of his cheeks, chin, and neck. She knew that kind of smoothness could only be achieved after a good clean shave. His cologne was enticing and

all she wanted to do was to reach out and cup his face into her hands. She wanted to pull him towards her, put her lips onto his, and kiss him for eternity. Disappointment set in when she found that she was not able to read his expression and this began to alarm her.

"What is this all about Tom?" she asked.
"I did some digging of my own and I found out a few things."
He looked upset and the atmosphere in the room began to get uncomfortable. Rising from his seat, he began to pace back and forth. Watching him intently, Kari nervously broke the silence.
"Tom," was all she could muster.
She started to get out of her chair to console him, but he walked away from her, putting distance between them.
"Kari, I'm not sure how to tell you this."
"Tell me what?"
She crossed the room towards him, not sure what was going on. This time she did manage to cup his face into her hands. Gently pulling him towards her, she placed her mouth on his. He didn't fight her, instead, he kissed her back. It was a kiss filled with passion. He hungered for her; he ached for her touch and her kisses. He just wanted to be near her. He did not want to let her go because — he knew he was falling in love with her.

It took every muscle in his body to pull himself away and yet somehow he managed to do it without making it so obvious that he needed to get away.
"Kari, please, can you sit down."
She leaned in for another kiss, but this time, he gently guided her back to her chair instead. Reluctantly Kari sat down, pouting like a child that was given a time-out for being bad.
"Alright, what is this all about? No more stalling — Let's have it," she demanded.
"You're right, no more stalling. OK, here it is. There is no good way to say this so, I'll just say it."
"Well, come on. You are just stalling now. Why don't you just start with — What this has to do with?"
"That's good. This has to do with your research."
"My research? You mean this has to do with Tess?"

"Yes, with Tess and Vie."

"Vie? What do you mean?"

Finally, he sat down next to her, took her hand into his, and began.

"Kari, did I ever tell you that I was raised by my grandfather?"

Shaking her head no, she couldn't recall him mentioning it before.

"Well, I was raised by grandfather because, when I was around four years old, both my parents had died in a car crash."

"Oh no Tom, I'm so sorry."

"I really don't remember much about them, but Pop, that's what I call him, had always tried to keep their memory alive — for my benefit.

I pretty much grew up in the cabin that I took you to see the other day. Pop and I had spent a lot of time out there, fishing, hunting, and just hanging around. Anyway, there was a time when I was seven or eight, I remember Pop taking me over to one of the neighbors on the lake. There was a huge bonfire and a bunch of grownups sitting around it. He had been taking me over there, from the time, when I started living with him. I really don't remember too awful much, but I do remember that while the adults drank and talked around the fire, I played in the dirt.

I gathered little pebbles and stones, then passed the time throwing them in the water. I don't know whose house it was that we were at, but I remember that the first bonfire of the summer was always the best. Every one of the lake people would be there and there would be tons of food to eat. I remember playing with a young girl once, but I never saw her again after that. Pop stopped taking me to the bonfires. I didn't think much about it back then because, I really didn't like going out there. I thought those bonfires were boring, except for the food part. Anyway, I think he used to sneak over there a time or two throughout the summer without me. Leaving me in the cabin alone, you know, when I was sleeping."

"So what does this have to do with Tess and Vie?"

"Vie's name stuck in my head. I thought that I had heard it before, so, I went to my grandfather last night to ask him if he knew her. The minute I mentioned her name, the color drained from his face. He wanted to know why I was asking about her. I knew then that he knew something. I asked him to tell me about her and through our conversation, I mentioned you.

I told him that I met an incredibly beautiful woman and that she loves to hear stories of the past. He wanted to know more about you, so I told him. I told him how we met and what you do for a living and then, I told him that I think I am falling in love with you."

Shocked by his last words, Kari's heart skipped a beat as she took an inaudible gasp. Still holding onto her hand, he began caressing it.

"Pops had become quite agitated and told me that I should not see you anymore."

"What? That is ridiculous. We are fully-grown adults here."

"Hang on, hear me out," he said as he gently squeezed her hand.

"Pop began to tell me a story. After my folks died, Pops took me in. As far as I know, I never had a grandmother; well, I never knew who she was. That little fact always bugged me as a child. There were pictures of Pop and me, pictures of me with my mom and dad and pictures of just my parents, but I never saw any pictures of my grandma. One day, when I got tall enough that is, I found a picture of a woman tucked away on the mantle. I asked him about her. He never revealed her name, he just said that she was the love of his life — the one that got away.

I didn't think much about it then, but now, after digging into this Tess's life, something has sparked an interest in me, an interest to find out more about my own past.

Pop told me that I never met this woman Vie; she died before I was born, but he certainly knows her. When I asked him about her, he told me that a long time ago he used to go to the prison to visit someone there. He used to bring some candies and a small amount of money that he would give to a woman prisoner."

Pausing for a moment, he looked Kari square in the face and said,

"I have to ask you something Kari. Do you know who your grandmother is?"

Thinking for a brief moment, she replied,

"Well... no, now that you mention it, I don't. I guess I never even thought about it. As a child, I was quite content with just my mother and Aunt Gert. They were all the family I ever knew and ever needed. You know, you can't miss what you never had, right? I mean, I never knew my father either. He ran out on my mom when she was pregnant with me so, meeting his side of the family was never an option. Why?"

"Just curious, I didn't know mine either, but I think I found her."

"What?"

"I think I found *my* grandmother."

"You're not making any sense," she said.

"Yeah, hear me out; back in 1947 Vie had already been in prison for a couple of years. I figured that out by her prison record. Pop told me that he used to go to the prison once a week and bring some sweets to a prisoner. He also gave some money to someone too."

"Alright... so what?"

"That was the same year that Tess was arrested for murder and subsequently went to prison."

"And...?"

"Pop went there to see Vie *and* Tess. He gave the sweets to Tess and the money to Vie. The money was to pay Vie to protect Tess because; *SHE* was the one that got away."

"How does that make her your grandmother?"

"Last night he told me about a woman that he loved a long time ago. They were both in their late teens. He used to cut her mother's lawn in the summer and plow the snow in the winters. He said, the moment he laid eyes on her, he was in love. He vowed to make her his wife. He worked hard and saved as much money as he could, in order to buy her a ring so they could wed, but her mother made it clear that she had other plans for her daughter.

That didn't discourage Pop, he would go over to her home, under the cover of darkness and they would have secret rendezvous in the late evenings. She would sneak out of the house and meet him out behind the barn on the far side of the flower garden. He said, her eyes twinkled in the moonlight and her face was as smooth as silk. She told him that her mom was getting ready to put her to work and that's when Pop decided to ask her to run away and marry him. She accepted his proposal and they planned to run away the next night. But that night, Pop's Pa suddenly died and he had to tend to his grieving mother and the funeral arrangements. He had no way of getting in touch with Tess to let her know. Unfortunately, by the time that the news had spread through the town about his father's passing, he learned that Tess had left without him.

He said he searched a long time for her, that he traveled many places trying to find her, but it was all in vain. He ended up joining the armed forces, where he served his country for a couple of years. That was where he met his best friend, Chuck. It was while he was on leave, his army buddy asked him to come out to his place because he was getting married. Chuck asked Pop to be his best man and he was elated. He told me that was a magical trip for him. Sure, he was happy that his friend was getting married, but what made it more exhilarating — he found Tess.

He said that he spent as much time with her as he possibly could, but when the wedding was over, Pop had to return to base. While he was getting his orders to ship out, she left the area and he lost her again. With his heart broken into a million pieces after losing her twice, he vowed never to look at another woman again. He had spent his entire life looking and waiting for her, but she never returned.

Then out of the blue, he had heard that she had a child. It was said that she couldn't take care of the baby, so she left it with Chuck and his wife. That would be my father. The couple kept the baby and raised him as their own.

Fast forward several years, my father grows up into a man and marries my mother. Soon after, I was born.

When I was only three and a half years old, my parents went out to the store; leaving me behind to stay with my grandparents. Not long after they headed out, there was a terrible accident, where they both died at the scene. It was after their funerals that I was suddenly uprooted and given away to Pop, my fraternal grandfather."

"I still don't get the connection. How is Tess *your* grandmother?"

"Pop told me that after the accident, Chuck's wife became very ill and unstable, she could no longer take care of me. That's why they called Pop."

"Oh no, that is just terrible."

"Don't you get it Kari? Why in heaven's name would this couple call Pop, *out of the blue*, to take me? I did some digging and I found out that Chuck had at least one sibling, a sister. I couldn't find out too much about his wife, but I really wasn't trying to either. But what really gets me is this, if they were my real grandparents, why wouldn't they just leave me with his sister, my aunt?"

Thinking about it and trying to fit the pieces together, Kari couldn't see the connection. Looking up at Tom, all she could do was shake her head and shrug her shoulders. Letting him know that she had no idea as to why any of that transpired.

"Here, maybe you'll understand better after I tell you this."

Moving to the living room, Kari curled up on the end of the couch where she sat in anticipation. Tom sat down next to her, took a deep breath, then he began to tell Kari a story.

"You know, when I was a kid, my Pop used to take me to the library and leave me there alone. He was never gone very long, maybe an hour or so. You know, I never thought much about it, until yesterday. I asked him about the trips to the library last night. I wanted to know where it was that he went when he left me there. Before he answered me, I saw his eyes swell up with tears. He finally told me that he used to travel to the old prison to visit with his love, of course, by that time it wasn't a prison any longer. He tried to convince her to come home with him, but she wouldn't budge.

He wanted to let her know how much he still loved her. So one day when he went to visit her, he asked her to marry him. On bended knee, with her hand in his, he proposed to her again. But this time she said no. It broke his heart, but it didn't stop him from visiting her once a week either. Then one day — it all stopped. He never went back to the old prison and I never went back to the library. After a few weeks of staying home, I asked him when we would be going back to the library. That was when he informed me there would be no more trips into town. I remember that very vividly, because I really did like going to the library. So, last night when I asked him why he stopped taking me to town, he told me that he stopped going because she — his love — had died."

Rising from her seat, Kari immediately leaned over to wrap her arms around his neck and gently give him a hug.

"Oh, Tom, I don't know what to say. What a heartbreaking story. I feel so bad for your grandfather. His whole life, waiting for and wanting only one woman and here she was — always just out of reach."

"I know. And now, I think I just opened up some fresh wounds for him. Before I left to come over here, I had seen him holding a picture of her and tears rolling down his cheeks."

"Did you tell him that Tess is still alive?"

"No."

"Why not? We have to tell him Tom."

"Not so fast Kari, I think that we, or better yet you, need to talk to Tess about this first. You need to find out why she wanted Pop to believe that she was dead. I think there is more to this story than the little bit of breadcrumbs that I just threw out."

Although, she was not particularly happy with what she just heard, she knew deep down that he was right. Besides, with Tess unwilling to speak, she had her work cut out for her now.

"You're right Tom, Monday I will begin a new strategy to see if I can break her from her silence."

With that, he took her into his arms and kissed her.

CHAPTER 40

Monday morning couldn't come quick enough. Kari had been preoccupied with thoughts of Tess, all weekend long. With much anticipation for her workday to begin, she bounced out of bed long before her alarm clock rang.

Pulling into the parking lot an hour before her shift, she entered the building and quickly headed for the locker room to change. Now that she was ready to start her day, she headed off to Tess's room.

As she stood outside of room 237, Kari took a deep breath to settle the slight nervousness that she felt. Lightly knocking on the door, she entered the room. She found Tess still in bed and sound asleep.

Not feeling right about waking her up so early, she went into the closet to pick out some clothes for Tess to wear for the day. As she mingled around the sparsely filled closet, she found the wooden box that she had come across several weeks before. She grabbed the box off the shelf and held it in her hands, just staring at it. Opening the box without permission is an invasion of one's privacy, but she wanted to know what was in there. Stealing a glance over her shoulder to see if Tess had awaken yet; she found that she was still fast asleep.

Teetering back and forth, as to whether or not to open the box, Kari's curiosity got the best of her. Slithering down the wall inside the closet to the floor, she slowly began to open the wooden box. As she lifted the lid and the contents inside started to come into view, the guilt of what she was about to do became too overwhelming. She closed the lid so quickly that it made a loud clanking sound. Her heart started racing and the beat was so loud in her ears, that she thought Tess would hear it. Stretching out her neck, she peered around the corner of the closet and once more found Tess lying peacefully in her bed, sound asleep.

With the box on her lap and her hands firmly on the lid, Kari fought with her moral dilemma. Telling herself that, if she opened the box and found any pictures, she could bring them out and ask

Tess to tell her about them. But, what if Tess didn't want her to see them. What if she opens the box and Tess didn't want anyone to know what was inside — she would then lose any trust that she had already built with her.

Slowly, her hand caressed the box lid and even though her fingers slightly lifted the lid, her heart told her not to do it. She knew she wasn't going to be able to open the box, at least not without permission. Content with her decision to not open the box, she started to get up from the floor, when she found Tess standing over her.

"Tess! Good morning, I didn't hear you get up."

She stood up quickly, still holding the wooden box in her hands, then said,

"Oh my goodness, I know what you are thinking. I didn't open it Tess. I promise you that I didn't. I won't lie to you, Tess. I was going to open it, but my heart wouldn't let me. I am so sorry."

Turning to put the box back on the shelf, Tess reached out and snatched it from her hands. She clutched the box firmly to her chest and walked back towards the table. Kari's heart fell to the pit of her stomach. *Now you've done it*, she thought. *She will never trust you again after this.*

Tess gently placed the box on the table and sat down in one of the kitchen chairs. After a few moments, she slowly turned to Kari and motioned for her to sit at the table too. Without hesitation, Kari went over to the table and sat down.

"Tess, please don't be mad at me. I didn't open the box. I knew it was wrong to go through your personal belongings without permission. In fact, I was going to bring the box out after breakfast and ask you if you would like to go through it."

There was no response from Tess. Kari was sure that if she had gotten her mad enough, surely she would try to say something. But Tess just remained as silent as ever, even though her eyes never left the box.

"I have a confession to make," she told her.

Tess's demeanor told her that she was listening.

"Remember how I told you about Tom, the new man in my life? Well, he has been helping me at the library and we had a few dinner dates over the past several weeks. Do you recall the stories I told you? The ones about John and Lucy? Well, I had been interested in knowing about you too. I had done some digging and I found out a few things. I really wish you'd speak to me about it, so that you can clarify some of the information I have."

Tess didn't move a muscle. She sat a still as could be, as if she was waiting for something.

"Tess, first I want to tell you that I think I finally met my soul mate. I think that I am in love with Tom, and I know that he loves me too — he told me the other day. I know what you're thinking; *why are you telling me this and what does this have to do with the box.'* Well I'll tell you. Through our digging, we believe that we found your grandchild."

Tess's back straightened quickly and her eyes lit up. Her fingers began to tremble against the box, that only moments before, were firmly gripping it. Kari noticed her reaction immediately and decided to press on.

"I know that you were a convicted felon, but from what I read Tess, I don't believe you did it. I want to hear it from you about what really happened, and I want you to meet your grandson."

Tess flinched ever so slightly, that Kari would never have noticed it. Slowly, she lifted the lid of the box and revealed the contents. Inside there was a stack of envelopes, neatly tied with a red ribbon, several old black and white photos, a single earring and oddly enough, a dried up carnation. Tess took the photo's out and one by one, she looked at the pictures and then passed them over to Kari.

The first photo was of two young girls standing side by side, smiling for the camera. There was no way of knowing who the girls were or where the picture was taken.

"How cute! Who are these girls, Tess?"

Saying nothing, she just passed along another photo. This one was of a beautiful woman, dressed in a smart looking suit with a matching hat, clearly an outfit from the '40's era. Upon further examination, Kari had deciphered who it was in the photo.

"Oh my Tess, this is you isn't it? You are absolutely, gorgeous. How old were you in this photo?"

Kari went back to the first photo and reexamined it, only to finally be able to recognize one of the two girls — Tess. She was posing with another girl, possibly her sister. Tess handed over yet another photo. This one was of a handsome young man. He was wearing overalls, a cap and posing next to a tractor. A name was penned on the back of the photo — Toby. Tess began to cry when she looked at the rest of the photos and that was when Kari decided not to push her any further. She took the remaining pictures from Tess's shaking hands and gently placed them back into the box.

"Tess we don't have to do this today. Come on, let's go outside and have our morning tea. You get dressed while I fetch the tea. Maybe I can scrounge up some biscuits or something to go with it."

Tess rose from her seat, shuffled over to the closet to retrieve some clothes, while Kari stepped out to get their tea and some goodies.

Kari returned with the goods and found Tess in her wheelchair ready to go.

"Man you're quick Tess. I can't even get ready that fast," she chuckled.

Handing over the two cups of tea and a small folded napkin, which contained a couple of shortbread cookies for each of them, Kari pushed her out onto the patio.

"It's going to be another beautiful day Tess. Don't you just love the scent in the air, fresh cut grass whispering by on a gentle morning breeze?"

Tess lifted her head into the breeze to smell the grass scent too. A smile crossed her face as she, too, captured the sweet fragrance of newly cut lawn.

As they sat on the patio sipping tea and eating their cookies, Tess brought out her wooden box that she had hid under her blanket. As she fumbled with trying to put it onto the table, Kari's quick reflexes saved it from falling onto the ground.

"Tess, there is no need to go through this box today. I do not want you to get upset. There will be plenty of time tomorrow or the next day. Let's just have a nice quiet time right now. Let's just enjoy the sunshine and the sweet song of the birds as they serenade us."

Kari spent the whole day with Tess, outside. She managed to get all of her meals brought out to the patio and they traveled the path in the yard at least four times. She talked endlessly about

Tom, telling her how smitten she is over him. Describing in detail how handsome and smart he is, and how happy she was that she found him to be a true gentleman.

Kari was careful with her words; she did not want to disclose too much information. Such as how turned on she gets when he is near, or how willing she is to forget that she is a lady and throw herself at him. How she aches for him to make love to her and, not to mention how the scent of his cologne drives her absolutely wild.

No, there will be no discussion in that general area. How awkward would that be anyway, letting a grandmother know how hot she is for her grandson? Sharing her deep sexual desires with her is probably not the best conversation to have — ever.

Kari physically shook her head to get those thoughts loose. The mere thought that Tess might know about her desires for Tom, seemed almost borderline incestuous.

The evening was soon approaching, as Kari gathered their belongings up before bringing Tess back inside. Carefully, she tucked the wooden box onto Tess's lap and covered it with the blanket. When she finished throwing out their trash and tidied up the patio, she brought Tess back inside to her room.

"Tess, you get yourself ready for bed and I'll put your box back into the closet, then I'll be back tomorrow."

Not wanting her to put the box away, Tess grabbed it from her hands, placed it on her bed, and put her hand firmly on top of it. This signified to Kari that she wanted to keep the box near her. Kari understood. She figured that Tess didn't trust her and thought she would sneak in and look through the box. Feeling sad that it had come to this, she said,

"OK Tess, I get it. I won't put the box in the closet. How about we put it on your nightstand instead?"

Carefully, Kari took the box and placed it on the nightstand. As Tess went into the bathroom to wash up for bed, Kari straightened up the room while she waited for her to come out.

Once she got Tess comfortably tucked into bed, Kari kissed her on her forehead then turned to leave. Tess grabbed at her hand to stop her then turned her head toward the box. Motioning for her to grab it, Kari picked up the box and handed it over. Slowly, Tess opened the box and pulled out a bundle of envelopes. Kari couldn't help but notice that there were two bundles of envelopes in the box. One bundle had a red ribbon tied around it, and the other tied in pink. Carefully, Tess placed the bundle with the pink ribbon back into the box, as she handed over the bundle with the red ribbon to Kari.

"What's this? Do you want me to read these?"

Nodding in approval, Tess turned out her lamp and rolled onto her side. She was telling her, *enough said!* Tess just dismissed Kari from her room.

CHAPTER 41

With a stack of old letters bound with a red ribbon, Kari climbed into bed hoping to get a few hours of reading in before drifting off to sleep.

Excited to get started, but not in a hurry to get to the end, Kari slowly and meticulously examined the stack of envelopes carefully before she dared to untie them. The paper that was once a brilliant white had yellowed over time and the once bright red ribbon had dulled over the years. As she flipped the stack over in her hands, a musty scent hovered in the air. It was similar to the scent that emanated from the boxes in the library's basement.

As she examined the top envelope, her eye drifted over to the postmark. The date stamped across the four-cent stamp in the corner was, Aug 21, 1962. Fanning through the rest of the stack, she noticed that all the dates were in reverse chronological order. The first letter that she received was on the bottom with the last and final letter on the top.

Kari was excited to start reading, not knowing what secrets she might learn. Holding her breath, she gently pulled the end of the ribbon. The bow came undone easily, as if Tess had tied it no more than a week ago. The ribbon slipped away from the envelopes and Kari carefully placed it on her nightstand, for safekeeping. She then took the bottom envelope and began to read. She read late into the night with no intension of stopping, that sluggish feeling that she had earlier, was now long gone.

All the letters began in the same sweet way, and obviously penned by the same individual. Although the penmanship was truly a work of art in its self, some words were hard to make out due to some of the writing was smudged and faded. The way the paper crinkled and yellowed in certain spots, led Kari to believe they were dried tear marks. The dried up tears that Tess must have shed while, reading the letters from her lover.

As Kari read each letter she, too, found herself welling up with tears. Oh, how this man loved her. As she read on, it seemed that he would have moved heaven and earth for her. But, in the end, when she needed him most, he couldn't do anything to help her out of her most difficult problem — going to jail for murder.

Reading each letter twice, Kari hoped to find out a little bit more about these two individuals. She wanted to make sure that she hadn't missed anything on the first pass. Each letter she read was filled with unconditional love and adoration towards her, but they seemed to be a bit vague. He didn't write about any specific day, a moment in time or even mentioned a location. His letters gave her the impression that he had been writing in code, saying things that only the two of them would know about.

She searched each letter looking for the mere mention of their child, but found none. She read each letter twice, looking for any mention of the murder or the time they had spent together. Of all the pages that she had read, she found no useful information. Even though Kari had learned how much this man loved Tess, she was still no closer to finding out anything new about her and that was disappointing.

Staring at the last page of the letter, Kari smiled at the closing that the writer wrote:

You are forever in my heart, until time no longer exists.
Always ready as the rain.
TW

CHAPTER 42

The sun was just beginning to rise. As it began to peek through the window blinds, the narrow rays beamed on Kari's face. Seeing the brightness through her closed eyelids, she began to stir awake. As the fogginess began to fade, she realized she had fallen asleep with Tess's love letters all over her bed. She was stunned to find that, she had fallen asleep while still holding onto the last page that she had read.

As she checked over the sheet paper in her hand, making sure that she didn't damage it while sleeping, her eye was drawn to the closing signature again. Studying the initials TW, Kari was stumped as to who TW could be. Suddenly she realized that she didn't even know what Tom's last name was, let alone his grandfather's. Without a second thought, she grabbed her phone.

Ring.....ring....ring. Ring....ring....ring.
After several rings a groggy, sleep filled voice finally answered.
"Hello."
"Tom? Did I wake you?"
There was a brief pause when she heard,
"No. I was just sitting up in bed at six-thirty in the morning, waiting for you to call me. In fact, I can't even recall going to sleep at all."
"I'm sorry Tom. I had no idea what time it was. I too just woke up, but I really have to ask you something."
"I sure hope it will be worth it for me" he paused. "Are you going to ask me if I would mind if you showed up here in nothing but your bathrobe? Because, if that's what you have planned for us then, I'm in and the answer is *YES!*"
"Well…. not exactly."
"I'm just messing with you sweetie, what do you want to ask me?"
Immediately a smile crept along her lips, when she heard him call her sweetie. A warm sensation filled her as she thought that things must be getting serious between them — he gave her a pet name. She wanted to dive deeper into their current conversation because, she loved listening to the suggestive way he would tease

her. Now she was having second thoughts about bringing up the real reason for the call. She didn't want to ruin the alluring and provocative mood that was beginning to take shape. As she contemplated playing in to his sexual fantasy, she heard,

"Kari — Honey are you there?"

Shaken back to reality, Kari answered, but not before she realized that she had suddenly begun to blush. Before she could think of something proper to say, her mouth decided to take over when her brain had a momentary lapse. In other words — she had a brain fart.

"Uh huh, I'm here. I was just imagining you lying in bed, while you're talking to me. That's all."

"Did you call me just to hear me talk to you while I was in bed?"

"Heavens no," she exclaimed, as her brain finally figured out that her mouth had run off on its own, thinking it knew better. Now her brain was working twice as fast to fix the trouble that her mouth had caused. "I called to ask you what's your grandfather's name."

"So, let me get this straight. First, you wake me up at six-thirty in the morning telling me you are fantasizing about me in bed and then you ask me about my grandfather? That's kind of... disturbing. What kind of weird sexual desires do you practice? Tell me, do I have to worry about losing you to my grandfather?"

"Thomas! What kind of woman do you think I am? I would never — hell I don't even know your grandfather."

"I'm just kidding with you," he said, followed by a short pause. Then he added, "OK, all kidding aside, my grandfather's name is Gene Wright. Why? What is so important that you needed to know this information right now?"

"Well, Tess gave me her love letters from a man that loved her to no end. I read them over and over again, but unfortunately I found nothing. I don't even have his name, he signed every letter the same way too — TW."

"What do you mean, she gave you her love letters?"

"Yeah, yesterday morning she caught me holding her wooden box and..."

Now fully awake and with peaked interest, Tom interrupted her in mid-sentence.

"A wooden box?" he asked. "What does that mean?"

"It means just that Tom, a wooden box! Every woman has a small wooden box that holds sentimental items they have saved over their lifetime."

"Oh, they do? Do you have a wooden box?"

"Never mind that, will you? Do you want to hear this or not?"

Thinking that he may have just jumped over the line and entered into the *forbidden zone*, where *hell hath no fury*, he quickly decided to try to appease this goddess of a creature on the other end of the phone.

"Alright, OK, I surrender. I won't interrupt anymore — unless of course I have a legitimate reason. Please continue," he said as pleasantly as possible.

"Thank you," she sighed. "Well, like I said before, she caught me holding her wooden box and when I told her that I didn't open it, which I didn't. She took it from me and opened it herself. I thought she was mad at me, but she ended up showing me a couple of pictures that she had inside of it. Then at the end of the day, she handed me a stack of letters that she wanted me to read."

"How do you know that's what she wanted? Did she tell you?"

"Not verbally, no. She just handed them to me, turned out her light, and then she just went to bed. I took the stack home and read them all last night. This morning was when I noticed that the closings on all of the letters ended the same way."

"How's that?"

"*You are forever in my heart, until time no longer exists. Always ready as the rain, TW.* Isn't that romantic?"

"Yeah, sounds very nice."

"Well, as I read through all the letters, I came to a conclusion."

"What conclusion?"

"I don't think that Tess is your grandmother. I found nothing in any of the letters referencing a child that they had together. Not to mention that the initials TW doesn't match up with your grandfather, Gene."

"Well, hang on a minute Kari; don't go discounting this so fast. When you asked me my grandfather's name, I only gave you his first name. His whole name is Eugene Tobias Wright. He used to go by the name Toby — back in the day, when he was young. So it very well could be him. TW could stand for Toby Wright."

This gave Kari pause. As she mulled over what Tom had just suggested, an idea occurred to her.

"I wonder if she ever wrote back?" she asked.

"What?"

"I wonder if Tess ever wrote back to your grandpa — how do you feel about asking him for his love letters."

"I don't think I would feel too good about that. That isn't something we guys do, you know."

Chuckling at the thought, she said,

"Oh, alright, but if you find that it may come up in a conversation....."

"If it ever comes to that Kari, I'll be all over it. Don't you worry — you can count on me."

Smiling at his sarcasm, Kari took a deep breath, and then quickly told him to meet her at work, before she quietly hung up the phone.

CHAPTER 43

Tess had gotten up early and dressed herself for the day. Once she finished tidying up her room, she went over to her favorite seat — the rocking chair. Once situated, she placed the wooden box on her lap and looked at it intently. Her eyes quickly shifted towards the clock that sat on the small table next to the window. Seeing that it was only five o'clock in the morning, she noted that she had at least two hours before anyone would check in on her. That gave her plenty of time to go through her personal things, without any nosey busybodies snooping around.

Sitting in the silence of her room, Tess stared at the box resting on her lap, and was now unsure if she wanted to open it. There were so many memories stuffed inside that, even after all these years she was frightened to revisit them. In the beginning, she only placed things inside that brought her joy and happiness. Wonderful memories that she wanted to save forever, but somehow, it ended up turning into a box full of sadness and regrets.

Her old and wrinkled fingers began tracing along the outline of the box, feeling the smoothness of the wood. As her hand moved along its edges, a small sliver of a smile began to form across her lips. She chuckled to herself, as a memory began to flood back to the forefront of her mind. She recalled the day that Toby, her lost love, had given it to her as a gift.

Toby, the love of her life, was a relentless and an extremely persistent young man. He was the type of man that wouldn't take no for an answer and he never gave up trying either. No matter how many times she refused his invitations to go to lunch, the movies, or a dance, he just kept on asking her. Finally, she relented and accepted his offer to carry her books from school. That was the beginning of their whirlwind love story.

As her mind tried to pinpoint exactly when everything started to go downhill, she felt her heart start to sink into the pit of her stomach. So many things had happened throughout her life that, it was hard to isolate the exact moment when things started going to hell in a hand basket.

Knowing that there was no way to travel back in time to fix or alter her past, the sadness began to consume her. As her trembling fingers caressed the lid, Tess dug deep within her soul to convince herself that she needed to open the box and reflect upon her past life in order to move forward.

Lifting the lid ever so slowly, she pulled out a bundle of letters tied with a pink satin ribbon. Holding them in her hand for a very brief moment, she hastily set them aside — for now. There was absolutely no reason for her to re-read those letters. She knew exactly whom they were from and what they said. She had no desire to re-visit that part of her past. At her age, there was no room in her heart for hate. And hate is exactly what would emerge, if she even so much as tried to open one of those letters.

Keeping them had never been her intentions, but it seemed safer to lock them away than to destroy them. Her biggest fear had always been that someone might find and read them, and then another world of problems would begin. Sure, she could have burned them once the halfway house became a nut house, but by then, she had all but forgotten that box was in the closet hidden away. In fact, it wasn't until she saw Kari holding on to it that she even remembered it existed.

Carefully, Tess took out the photos that she had shown to Kari earlier and fondly gazed upon them. Smiling at the picture of the two young girls, she remembered the day that picture was taken; it was the day she was to run away and elope. The next photo was of a striking young man. Standing tall in his dust-covered overalls, posing next to the tractor he used in the fields. He was still the most handsome man that she had ever met. Seeing his picture brought tears to her eyes and soon she began to weep. *Oh, why did I ever let him go? What a fool I was and still am*, she thought. *So many years wasted, and for what?* As her old and wrinkled fingers caressed the picture of her love, Tess could no longer bear it — finally allowing herself to break down, she began to cry.

Tears streamed down her cheeks, leaving little wet, slick marks as they fell. Soon a puddle began to form on her lap and her tears began to dampen her clothing. Sixty-plus years of pent-up tears that streamed from her eyes, were now free to flow. With nobody left in her life to force her to stop crying, she found that there was absolutely no reason to hold back any longer either. All the tears her dear friend prevented her from shedding were now, flowing like a small river's waterfall on a calm spring day.

Drying her eyes as best as she could, Tess looked inside the box again, this time she pulled out a paper-clip that had two keys strung on it. Carefully, she held them up in front of her eyes, thoroughly examining them. Slowly, she wrapped her fingers around them, until they were completely clasped into the palm of her hand and no longer visible. Clutching them to her chest, more tears began to pool in her eyes. She halfheartedly tried to not let the tears fall, but her lids could no longer hold them back, and they too began flowing down her soft delicate cheeks.

Drying her eyes for a second time, she gently set the keys on her lap and peered into the box for a third time. Lying on the bottom was a white envelope. She didn't need to open it, because she knew exactly what was inside. Everything that she owns is in that envelope and for the first time in her life, she knew exactly what to do. The best part was, finally there was nobody left to tell her any different.

Picking up the paper clipped keys, Tess slipped them into the white envelope. She then took the picture of the handsome young man, wrote something on the back of it and slipped that too into the envelope. After careful consideration, she took the other pictures, jotted something on the back of them, and slid them inside as well.

As she started to placing things back into the box, she noticed a few small miscellaneous items that had trickled to the bottom. There was a brass button, an old movie ticket stub, one earring, and a single dried rose. She picked each of these items up and gently ran her fingers caressingly over them. As she held each piece in her hand, a tidal wave of emotions came flooding over her as the memories came to her mind. Spending considerable time with each item, she secretly wished she could somehow turn back the hands of time. She cherished the memory that each piece brought forth, but her heart was confused on whether to be happy or sad. She relished in all the memories, but when she thought about all her missed opportunities and wrong turns that she had made throughout her life, her heart broke.

Carefully she began to place the items back into the box, starting with the stack of letters secured in the pink ribbon. Once they were in position, she gathered all the smaller items — the ticket stub, the brass button, the single earring, saving for last, the dried rose.

Now that she had put everything neatly away, she picked up the plain white envelope and placed it on top of everything else. She wanted it to be the first thing anyone would see, upon opening the box. Hoping that whoever it may be, they would open the envelope first.

Ever so gently, Tess closed the lid of her precious wooden box. The moment she heard the soft sound of the two piece's latching closed, sealing the items inside, a small piece of her heart died away.

CHAPTER 44

Arriving at work as scheduled, Kari parked her car near the end of the first row. As she cut the engine of her car, she began surveying the parking lot hoping that she could spot Tom. *Maybe hanging up on him, before he could respond, was a bad idea*, she thought. Not sure if he was coming, but ready to start her shift, she gathered up her belongings and exited her car. Scanning the parking lot one last time, she headed off towards the building. As she was about to grasp the door handle, she heard,

"Whoa, Kari, wait up a minute."

Recognizing the voice immediately and even before a smile could appear on her face, a warm feeling wrapped around her like a warm fuzzy bear hug. Turning toward the source of the voice, she said,

"You made it. I'm so glad that you came."

Tom was all but running from the parking lot to catch her before she entered the building. As he met her at the door, he planted a quick warm kiss on her lips, then said,

"Why did you ask me to meet you here? Don't you have to work today?"

"Yes, I do. But I have an idea."

"What kind of idea?"

"You'll see. Come on, I've got to get in before I'm late."

Grabbing his arm, they entered the Whispering Creek facility.

She completed her morning rituals while Tom waited patiently in the dining hall, when she finally asked him accompany her to room 237.

"Where are we going?" he whispered.

"You'll see. Come on, you can trust me."

Kari lightly knocked on the door before she entered the room. Taking a quick survey of the room, she had seen that Tess was already up and dressed for the day. She slipped her hand into Tom's and led him into the room, instructing him to sit at Tess's dinner table.

"Good morning Tess. I brought someone to meet you."
Tess, who had been rocking in her rocker, suddenly stopped. The look on Tom's face was complete shock. He had no idea that Kari would ever put him in such an awkward position as this. Seeing the old woman in the rocker, who had abruptly stopped rocking when she too heard the news that there was company, was enough to let him know — he was not alone in his feelings.

Kari also had sensed a moment of awkwardness that filled the air, but before she would allow that moment to take over, she pressed on.

Walking towards her charge, she stood in front of her, just as Melva did when she first met her, and said,
"Tess, I have something I want to share with you."
Taking a seat across from her, she took Tess's hand into her own and gently began to caress it.
"Tess, do you remember my first day here? Do you remember us going for a walk out back and me telling you the stories about John and Lucy?"
Tess raised her eyes to meet Kari's and ever so slightly, she nodded her head.
"Good. Now Tess, I told you those stories in hopes to get you to open up to me about your life and share *your* story. I know that you stopped speaking a long time ago and I still don't know why, but the more time that I spent with you, made me want to know about you more."
A thin smile appeared on Tess's face as she listened intensely to the words coming from Kari's mouth.
"Tess, I had been doing some research on you and I must say, what I have learned is amazing. You are a trooper, that's for sure. Unfortunately, I haven't learned anything about your youthful days; actually, the only thing that I have found was, what brought you to this place. You know, before it was Whispering Creek."
Tess took a deep breath and straightened her back, signaling that she was not comfortable with this conversation any longer. Reading her body language, Kari gently squeezed Tess's hand and continued.
"It's OK Tess; I've read and re-read your police record and the court transcripts. There is nothing in there that proves that you

ever did anything wrong, let alone kill anybody."

For a brief moment Tess had relaxed her posture, but she was not sure where Kari was going with any of it. As she sat in her rocker, her eyes remained locked on Kari's face.

Looking deep into Tess's eyes, Kari took a deep breath and decided to plunge forward to point of no return. She knew that one of two things would happen; either Tess would be delighted to have finally someone she could share her story with, or she would feel a deep sense of invasion of her privacy that she would never trust her again.

Glancing over Tess's shoulder, Kari found her strength renewed when she saw Tom sitting at the table, listening to her too. Mustering up her courage, she continued.

"Tess, all my life I have listened to stories. Many people have shared lifetimes of stories with me and I have spent my entire life, always wanting more, just like a junky. I never seemed to have time in my life to meet someone special or maybe I just never wanted to. Last night was when I came to know this about myself. It was because of the letters that you gave me. After reading them, I learned that TW loved you so much and yet, you managed to keep him at bay. I don't understand why you did that and what's more, it made me take a good hard look at my own life.

I too had managed to push everyone away from me, keeping everyone an arm's length. I never wanted to have someone take my attention away from what I thought was, my life's work. I believed that they would be better off not waiting for me to make time for them, because to tell you the truth, I never would have. I only ever wanted to hear stories of others. I lived my life through their stories and before I knew it, my own youth had slipped away."

Kari could feel that Tess had relaxed a little and that she too longed to hear what Kari had to say.

"I want you to know Tess; I will not give up on you. I want to know your story and I want to *hear* it from you. I know that you can talk if you want to and I am prepared to do what I have to, to get you to talk."

Standing up, Kari started to walk towards Tom as she said,

"So, with that being said Tess, I brought your grandson here to meet you."

Taking Tom by the hand, she led him over towards Tess. Together, they both stood before her. The look of shock was clearly written all over Tess's face and never once did it occur to her that, surprising an elderly woman in her nineties, could result in a heart attack.

Immediately Kari knelt down next to Tess, checking to see if she was all right. After a minute or two, which felt like forever, Tess began to breathe normally.

"Oh my goodness Tess, you gave me quite a scare. I'm sorry that I frightened you and I probably shouldn't have done it this way, but I think that you two needed to meet."

Tom not sure of what to make of everything, did what he does best. Bending down and taking her hand into his, he smiled at her and said,

"Hi Tess, I'm happy to finally meet you."

Tess said nothing. Another awkward moment filled the air as she just simply stared at his face. This time, though, Tom took the lead and broke the silence in the room.

"Tess, my name is Tom. Thomas Wright and I am the grandson of Gene Tobias Wright. I don't know for sure if you are the woman that had captured my grandfather's heart for eternity, but I sure would like to find out."

Upon hearing Toby's name, Tess warmly smiled back.

Kari sensed that the tension in the room was dissipating and began to move the wheelchair over to the rocker. She then asked Tess if she would like to go outside on the patio to have her tea. Without hesitation, Tess stood up with Tom's assistance and moved from one seat to the other.

Kari asked Tom to push Tess out to the garden area, while she went to get their tea. Moments later, they were all sitting on the patio, sipping tea and listening to the morning songs of the birds merrily chirping away.

Tom couldn't help but stare at the elderly woman. Seeing her picture on his grandfather's mantle hadn't made it any easier for him either. Try as he may, he just couldn't feel any connection towards the woman. *Well, you idiot! That is understandable. You never knew her, let alone known of her*, he thought. Trying hard to find something to talk about, he opened his mouth and said,

"Tess, I think there is a picture of you on the mantle. My grandfather never mentioned who it was in the photo, but after looking at your facial features, I really think it is you. I'll have to ask him, when I get home that is."

Tess gasped when he said that, then her look deepened as she stared long and hard at him. Not certain of what just happened, Tom turned to Kari and asked,

"What's wrong? Kari, what just happened here?"

"I'm not sure. Tess, what's the matter, are you OK? Did Tom say something wrong?"

Tess's heart began to race, she wanted to scream from the bottom of her lungs, but nothing would come out. So many years of silence had taken its toll and now when she needed it most, her vocal chords went into hiatus. She searched Tom's face, then quickly turned to Kari — her head moving back and forth, hoping that one of them would understand her. She knew that her look of desperation was not helping the situation at all. Trying with all her might, she sat back struggling to relax. Hoping that once she settled down, one of them would start talking again. It wouldn't take long, *Kari never disappoints*, she thought to herself. And as if on cue, Kari began to speak.

"Tess, I know you never really got to know your son, but this man sitting before you, looks just like him." Turning towards Tom, she then said,

"Tom, why don't you tell her a little bit about you and of your past?"

Clearing his throat, Tom sat a little taller in his seat and began telling her what little he remembered of his youth and of his father. As he neared the end of his story, he started talking about his grandfather again.

"And it was just a couple of days ago that he finally confessed, that all those times that he left me alone in the library, he was visiting someone that was in jail. I know that speaking of it makes you uncomfortable, and I'm really sorry about that. But what I do know Tess is this, my grandfather has loved only one woman his entire life and I believe that, that woman is you. He never married and as far as I could tell, he never even had a girlfriend. When I asked him who the woman in the photograph on the mantel was, his only reply was; *'she was the one that got away.'"*

Watching Tess's body language, it confirmed his suspicions. She was the *love* of his grandfather's life. Then he managed to muster up the courage to ask her a question,

"Tess, I'd like to ask your permission to tell my grandfather that I not only found you, but that I have met you as well. Would you give me your blessings to allow me do so? I know it would mean the world to him to know that you are still here, because his love for you never died."

Tess's eyes swelled with tears and a huge lump grew in her throat. She so badly wanted to speak to this man, there was so much that she wanted and needed to say. But, all she could manage was to nod in agreement and let her tears flow freely from her eyes.

CHAPTER 45

Seeing Tom off after the three had lunch, Kari spent the rest of the day just talking away to Tess. She told her that Tom was a wonderful man and that for the first time in her life, she believes that she may be falling in love. Soon she began to reveal her fantasy of the future, by saying that if she happened to marry him, then she would become her granddaughter too.

"Oh Tess how fun would that be, us being in the same family?"

Smiling with approval, Tess allowed Kari to continue with her busybody chattering. After all, Tess loved hearing her talk.

As Kari chattered on, Tess slowly sauntered over to her rocking chair and began to rock. Kari focused on cleaning up their dinner mess and tidied up the room. Before she knew it, the end of her shift had finally come. Even though it was an eventful day, Kari was sure that it had taken its toll on Tess. Too much excitement, all in one day, is not a good combination for the elderly — no matter how healthy and fit they may seem.

Looking at the clock on the wall, she went over to Tess and said,

"Tess, it's getting late and my shift is just about over. Come on, it's time for you to get up out of this chair and let me help you get ready for bed."

Tess rose from her rocker and holding on to Kari's arm, she let her lead her to the bathroom where she could change into her nightclothes. While she was in the bathroom changing, Kari had gone back over to the rocker where she had last seen Tess's wooden box. Picking it up, she once again had the urge to open it, but this time she managed to fight the impulse and resisted the temptation. *If she wants me to know what is in this box, she will tell me to open it*, she thought to herself. She placed the box onto the nightstand next to Tess's bed, as Tess came out of the bathroom.

"Tess, I straightened up your newspaper, removed all the trash from around your chair and I placed your box right here on the nightstand. You have a fresh bottle of water and I turned off your alarm. There is no need for you to wake up so early tomorrow, besides, you had a lot of excitement today. I think that you really need to have a good night's sleep tonight."

After helping Tess into her bed and smoothing out the covers, Kari laid her robe at the foot of the bed. She then positioned Tess's slippers right where her feet could slip right in, when she gets out of bed.

With Tess all settled in for the night, Kari leaned over and kissed her on her forehead. As she started to leave, she said,

"Good night Tess, I hope you have sweet dreams tonight."

Smiling down at her, she turned away from the bed to leave the room when, she added,

"One of these days Tess, I want to hear you tell me *your* story. I want to hear your voice and learn about your life first hand — from you! You've got a story, Tess — one that made you who you are. I know you can talk because, you used to. I just want you to try to find that voice once more — before it's too late. I know you will talk again — when you are ready."

As she turned to leave, Tess stretched out her hand and grabbed Kari's arm. With tears in her eyes, she opened her mouth to speak. As much as she tried, all that she could muster was nothing more than a dry crackled whisper. It wasn't much, but she did speak. Finally, after more than twenty-five years, Tess said,

"I'm as ready as the rain."

_ * _ * _ * _ * _ * _ * _ * _ * _

AUTHORS NOTE

I hope you enjoyed reading this book, and I would like you to know, that this is the first book I have ever written. Although it had taken me quite a while to compile, this book came to me one morning while washing my face. It was a true epiphany of sorts, because the entire story played in my mind from beginning to end, in less than a blink of an eye.

If you enjoyed Echoes of the Past — Westward Ho Series, then I encourage you to read the second book, Ready as the Rain — Westward Ho Series. Where Tess's dirty little secrets start to unfold. Find out if Kari's love will continue to bloom, or will it wither away into the nothingness that she had come accustomed to. There is so much more of this story to tell, but I do not want to ruin it for you here. Get *Ready as the Rain*, when it comes out and I promise you, you will not regret it.

You can find more information on my Facebook page, just go to: www.facebook.com/RM RadtkeAuthor. I would love to hear from you.

~RM Radtke

PS
I may be a new author, but I assure you that all authors will agree with me on the following. No matter what book you read, an author would appreciate a review — always.

ABOUT THE AUTHOR

RM Radtke is a first time author. She has been happily married for 27 years to her wonderful husband, Larry. Together, they have four children, one daughter, three sons, and two wonderful grandchildren.

As a full time office administrator, it's a wonder she can find time for anything else. Her love for writing stems back to her childhood, where she wrote poetry to convey her feelings. But, after writing several family eulogies, family members had strongly suggested she focus her talents into story writing and write a book.

Born and raised in Michigan, she is always ready for a spontaneous road trip. To her; the destination isn't the goal – the journey along the way is. Along with her passion for writing, she enjoys reading (when she can find the time) and evening walks with her husband (during the few warm months Michigan has to offer). When she's not working at her day job, or at home on her laptop writing, she is usually savoring a hot cup of coffee with her husband at either the local Tim Horton's or out back on her patio.

Follower her on Facebook at:
https://www.facebook.com/RMRadtke
Twitter: @RMRadtke_Author